W9-CJC-108

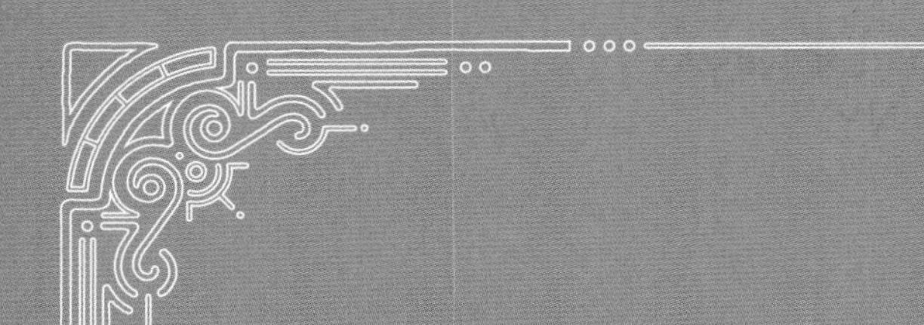

CREATED BY

JOHNNIE CHRISTMAS *and* JACK T. COLE

Writer **JOHNNIE CHRISTMAS**

Artist **JACK T. COLE**

Letterer **JIM CAMPBELL**

Editor **STEPHANIE COOKE**

Designer **BEN DIDIER**

Wordmark Logo **RIAN HUGHES** *Production Artist* **RYAN BREWER**

TARTARUS, VOL. 1. First printing. September 2020. Published by Image Comics, Inc. Office of publication: 2701 NW Vaughn St., Suite 780, Portland, OR 97210.

ISBN: 978-1-5343-1603-4.

IMAGECOMICS.COM

TARTARUS

VOLUME ONE

AS ABOVE / SO BELOW

CHAPTER ONE

BAXNAN/JURIAN WAR

9TH CYCLE

OLYMPUS STARCHART

{Long Moon discrepancies noted}

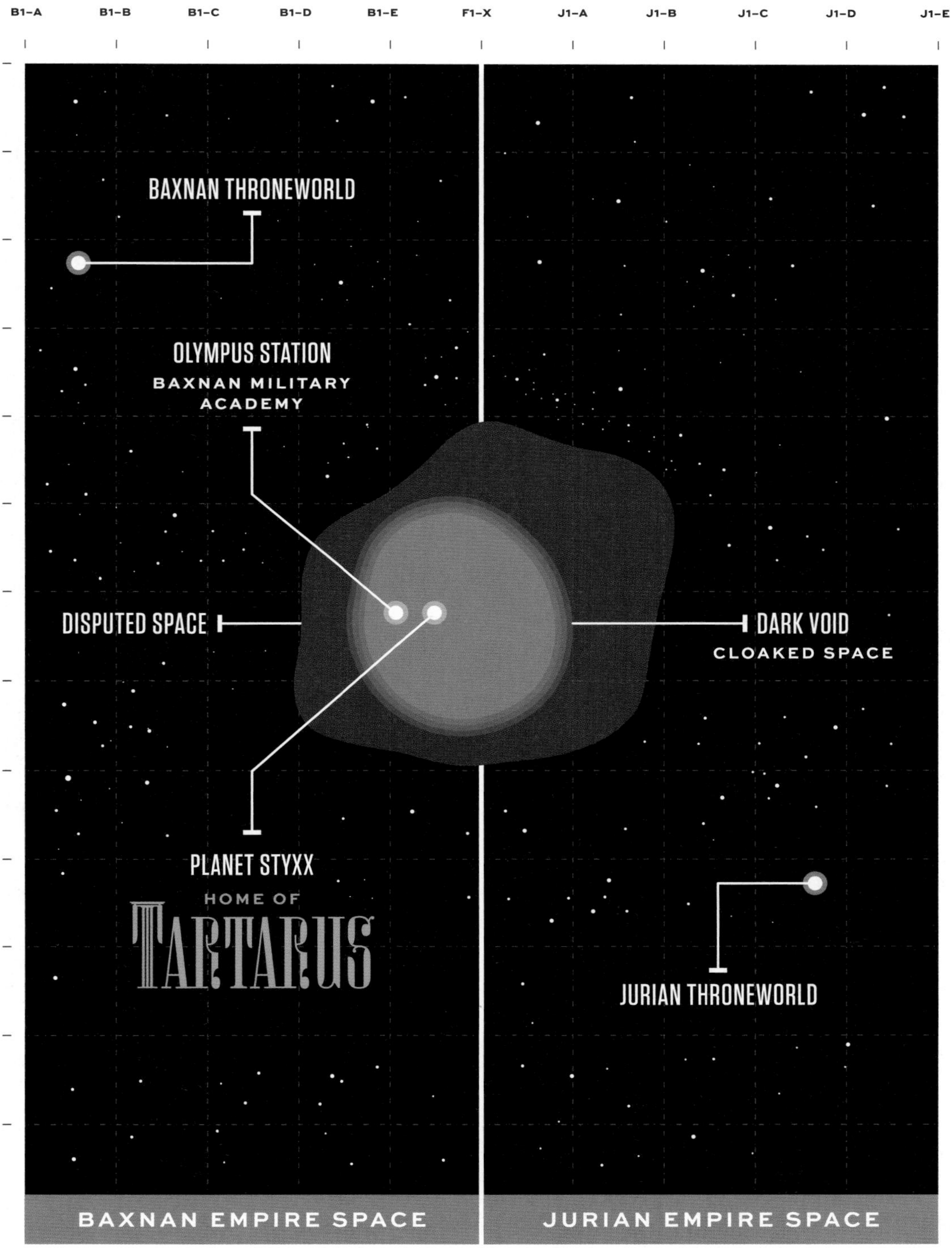

B1–A B1–B B1–C B1–D B1–E F1–X J1–A J1–B J1–C J1–D J1–E

BAXNAN THRONEWORLD

OLYMPUS STATION
BAXNAN MILITARY ACADEMY

DISPUTED SPACE

DARK VOID
CLOAKED SPACE

PLANET STYXX
HOME OF
TARTARUS

JURIAN THRONEWORLD

BAXNAN EMPIRE SPACE

JURIAN EMPIRE SPACE

“THE PIT” PRISON SCHEMATI

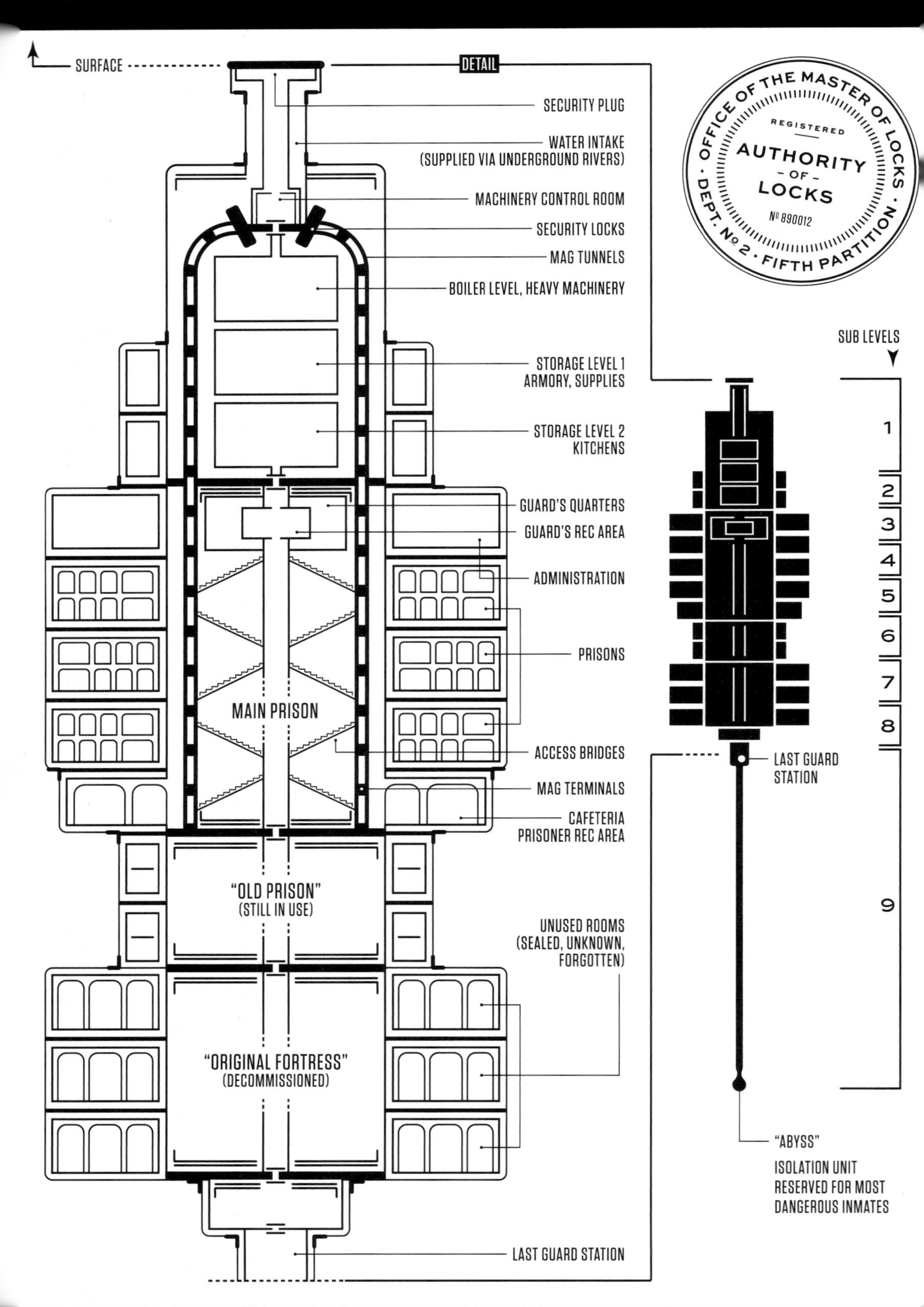

ROPERTY OF THE OFFICE OF THE MASTER OF LOCKS. DO NOT COPY. MUST BE SURRENDERED ON DEMAND. FAILURE TO COMPLY WILL RESULT IN IMMEDIATE PUNISHMENT TO THE FULLEST EXTENT OF TH

ART ONE: BELOW

THE PIT. MAXIMUM SECURITY UNDERGROUND PRISON.
NINE MILES BELOW TARTARUS.
"AS ABOVE, SO BELOW...STARS IN YOUR BELLY, STARS IN THE SKY..."

WHERE'D YOU HEAR THAT, TONZ?
I READ IT IN TODAY'S MEAL PACK. "THE DAILY INSPIRATION."
FLICK
XIII

SUB LEVEL 9.
THOSE "MEALS" ARE BARELY PASSABLE AS FOOD. NOW THEY'RE PUTTING GARBAGE IN YOUR HEAD TOO?
I GOT YOU SOMETHING.
IF YOU HAD ANY SENSE YOU'D QUIT. THAT PLACE IS GONNA GIVE YOU A HEART ATTACK!
DID'JA HEAR?

SAID I GOT YOU SOMETHING. IT'S PRETTY, JUST LIKE YOU.
DID YOU STEAL IT?
C'MON BABY, DON'T WORRY ABOUT--
TONZ. PRISON GUARD.

YOU'LL LOSE YOUR JOB...YOU NEED THAT JOB, TONZ--
A MINUTE AGO YOU WANTED ME TO QUIT.
ANYWAY, NOBODY'S GONNA CARE. I GOT IT OFF'A SURKA.
SURKA?! THE MURDERER?! SHE'S A MANIAC, TONZ!

SHE'S A PRISONER. AND I SAY SHE DON'T NEED PRETTY JEWELRY.
SHE'S LUCKY I DON'T SHOOT HER.
SURKA. PRISONER. WARLORD (FORMER).

URK--!
THAT DOESN'T BELONG TO YOU, TONZ! I'M SAVING IT FOR A SPECIAL SOMEONE.
SURKA?!
...TONZ?
BUT I DON'T WANNA LEAVE YOU EMPTY-HANDED...

I'LL TRADE YA.
I'LL TAKE THIS...

AND YOU TAKE MY CELL. THE COLD, DARK PLACE FILLED WITH FLESH-EATING WORMS.
TONZ, YOU ALRIGHT?!
SURKA! PLEASE--

KLOK
ARRRRGGHHH!
TONZ!

TONZ!
I WON'T BE NEEDING IT ANYMORE.

SUB LEVEL 8.
TOK
TOK
DID'JA HEAR THAT?

PROLLY JUST A COMPRESSOR--

UUHHNN!
WHUDD!
WHAT THE--?
KRAK.

DAMMIT!
THE ELEVATOR SWITCH IS LOCKED!

RRRAAAAA!

FREEEZE!
DON'T. YOU. MOOOOVE.

PIT COMPLEX KONTROL, COME IN. OVER.
READING YOU 952A. OVER.
GOT A FLEEING TROG--UM, PRISONER, ON SUB LEVEL 8.008. ONE GUARD DOWN. REQUESTING BACKUP. OVER

SHOOT PRISONER ON SIGHT. OVER.
CUT ME A BREAK, KONTROL! SHE'S HUGE! I'LL HAFTA' DRAG HER CARCASS AROUND ALL SHIFT. CAN I SHOOT HER AT CLOCK-OUT? OVER.

ON SIGHT, 952A. OVER.
GRUNT
COPY THAT.
ALRIGHT, DON'T MAKE THIS HARDER THAN IT HAS TO BE.
STEP INTO THE LIGHT...

UNLOCK THE ELEVATOR AND I'LL GRANT YOU A QUICK DEATH.

...SURKA?!

PHAMM
PHAMM
KONTROL, IT'S SURKA! SHE'S OUT OF THE PIT!

SHOOMP
THANKS.
DID YOU SAY "SURKA"?! OVER.
SEND HELP! OVER!
RNING!
DO NOT OPERATE ELEVATOR WITHOUT

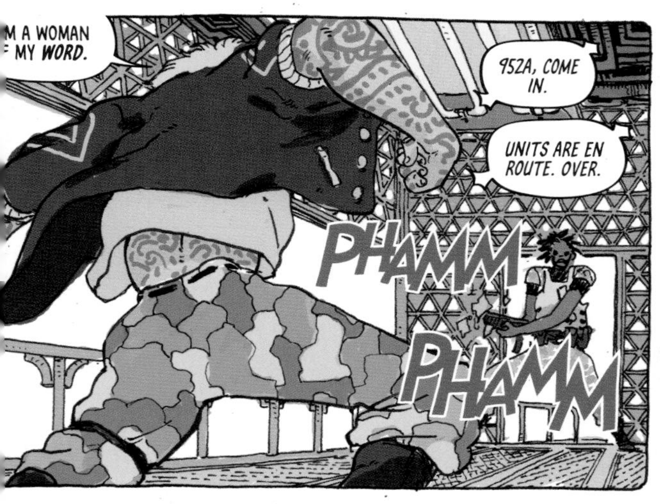
M A WOMAN
F MY WORD.
952A, COME IN.
UNITS ARE EN ROUTE. OVER.
PHAMM
PHAMM

WHAT'S YOUR STATUS? OVER.
UNNNGH!

952A...?

CRASH

WUUD

OVER...?
WHIR POP WHINE

WHEEEEEEP
WHEEEEEEP
WHEEEEEEP

MASTER OF LOCKS, HISA IKEDA'S QUARTERS.
WARDEN OF THE PIT.
BRUXISM...
IT'S JUST A FANCY WAY OF SAYING I GRIND MY TEETH.
MY JOB? HA, NICE TRY! OUR FAMILY IS FAR MORE STRESSFUL THAN RUNNING A PRISON!
STANDBY

SORRY, MA. I DIDN'T MEAN THAT.

HOW'S DAD?

I'LL COME SEE HIM TONIGHT. AFTER MY SHIFT. I PROMISE.

MA, I GOTTA CALL YOU BACK--
WHEEEEEEEP
WHEEEEEEP
WHEEEEEEP
MASTER OF LOCKS REPORT TO CONTROL CENTER! SURKA HAS ESCAPED FROM THE PIT. I REPEAT...

CELLBLOCK I
SURKA HAS ESCAPED...!

AND SHE'S NOT ALONE...

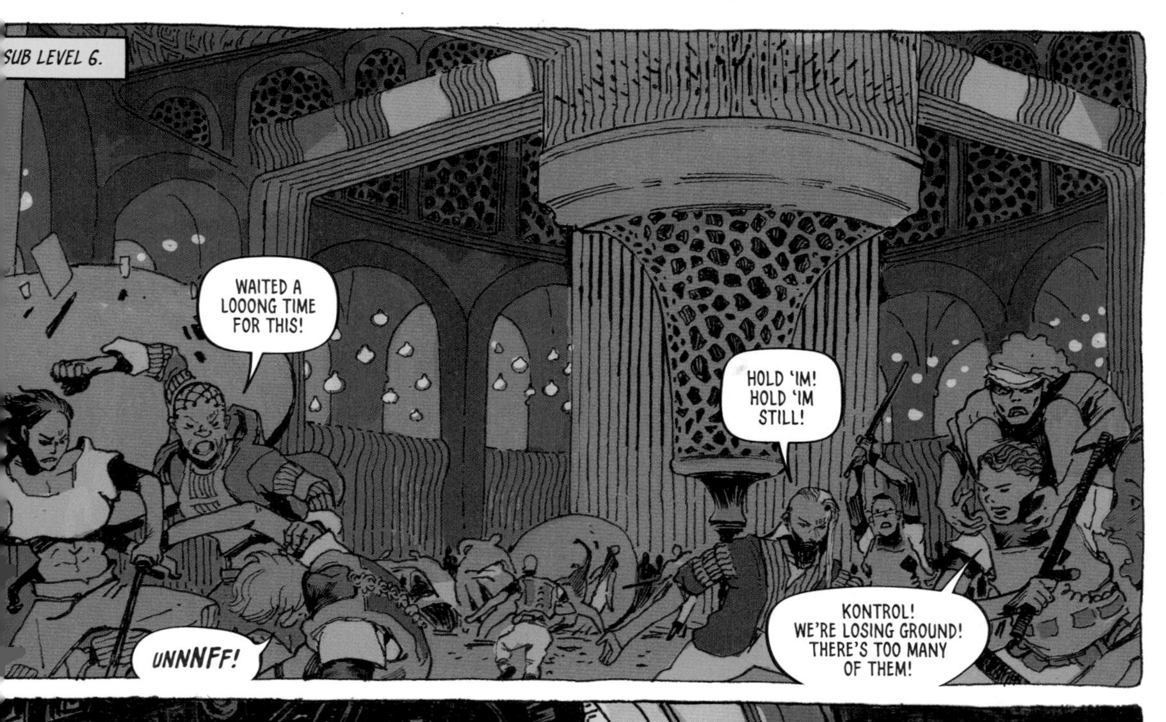
SUB LEVEL 6.
WAITED A LOOONG TIME FOR THIS!
HOLD 'IM! HOLD 'IM STILL!
UNNNFF!
KONTROL! WE'RE LOSING GROUND! THERE'S TOO MANY OF THEM!

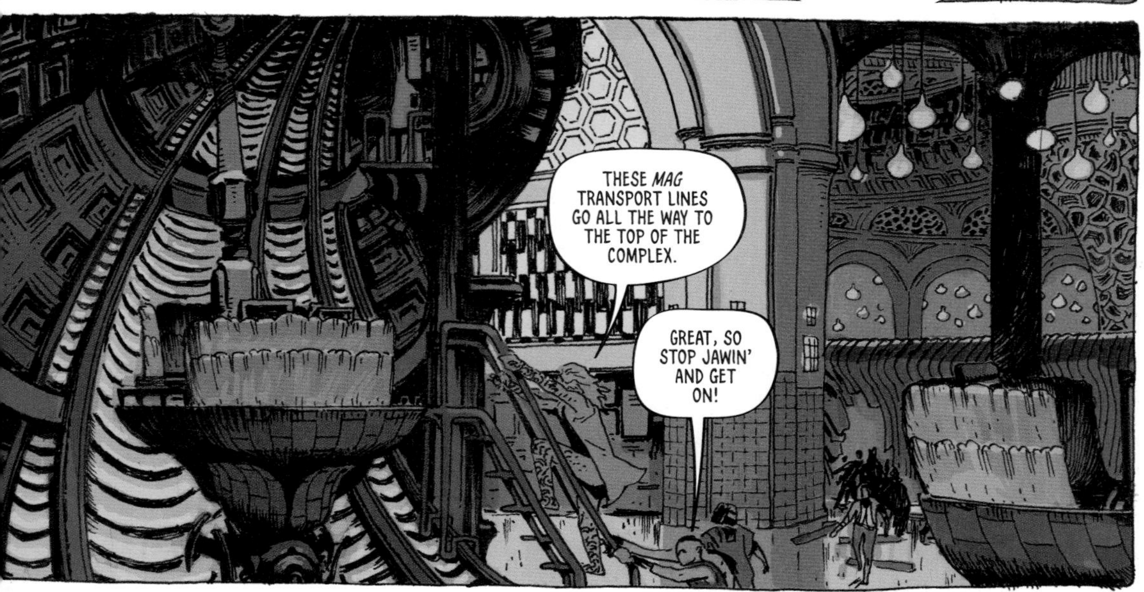
THESE *MAG* TRANSPORT LINES GO ALL THE WAY TO THE TOP OF THE COMPLEX.
GREAT, SO STOP JAWIN' AND GET ON!

AT THIS RATE, WE'LL BE HOME FOR BREAKFAST!
MAKE MINE A DOUBLE ON THE ROCKS!

PIT COMPLEX KONTROL. THE PIT'S OPERATION CENTER.
STATUS REPORT!
WE'VE GOT THREE PACIFIERS EN ROUTE.
PIT COMPLEX KONTROL TO MAG PACIFIER XU4. HAVE YOU ENGAGED THE ESCAPEES? OVER.

MAG PACIFIER XU4. WHAT IS YOUR STATUS? ARE THE PRISONERS CONTAINED? OVER.

SSSSS...

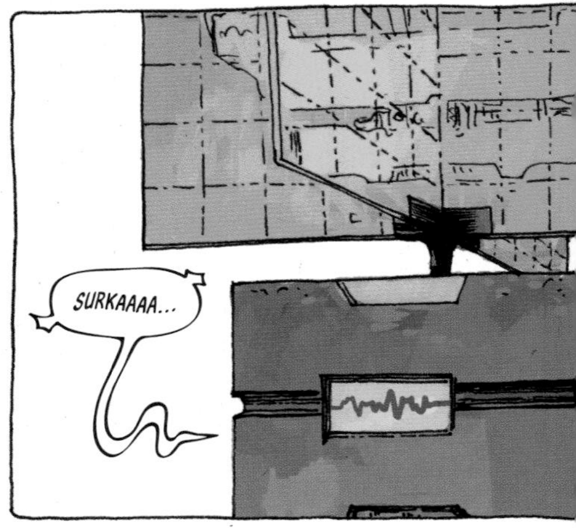
SURKAAAA...

SURKA THE TERRIBLE. THE UNCONQUERABLE. THE LEFT-HANDED WOMAN...

DAMN. THEY

SURKA, BAPTIZED IN WOE. TAMER OF TARTARUS. THE SMASHER OF BONE...

WE'LL NEVER GET OUT OF HERE...
CAREFUL...
...SHE IS THE DARK MOON.

NO ONE'S EVER--
GET *OFF* MY TRANSPORT!
AAAIIEEEEE!

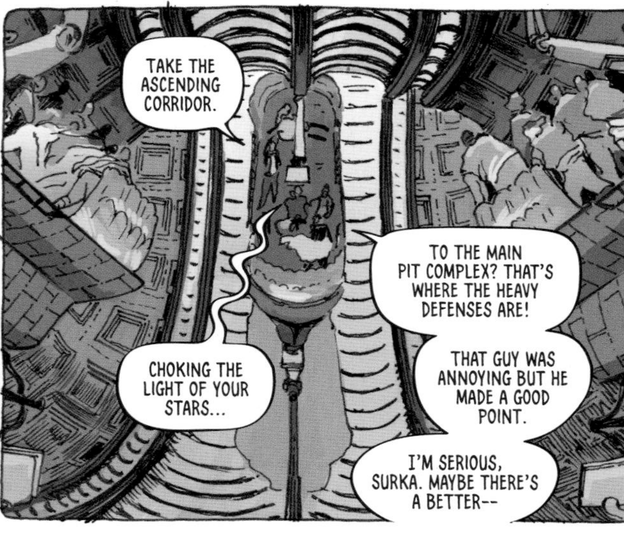
TAKE THE ASCENDING CORRIDOR.
TO THE MAIN PIT COMPLEX? THAT'S WHERE THE HEAVY DEFENSES ARE!
CHOKING THE LIGHT OF YOUR STARS...
THAT GUY WAS ANNOYING BUT HE MADE A GOOD POINT.
I'M SERIOUS, SURKA. MAYBE THERE'S A BETTER--

WE LEAVE *NIGHT*, SLIV! AYING IT SAFE" EANS WE *DIE* HERE!
YOU RATHER *DIE* SAFE OR *LIVE* DANGEROUSLY?
AS YOUR HOPES DROWN IN A WELL...

DO I HAVE A CHOICE?
...OF NEVER-ENDING SORROW.

SUB LEVEL 3.
WHAT THE--!
KONTROL, THE PRISONERS HAVE MADE IT TO SUB LEVEL 3. THEY'VE ENTERED THE MAIN COMPLEX!

WHY WOULD THEY COME INTO THE MAIN COMPLEX? IT'S SUICIDE.
AND TURN THAT MAG COMM *OFF!*
ON IT.
KLIK
SHE. IS. COMIN-- KSHHHHZZ
BOSS. THEY'VE GOT THE ACCELERATOR.

UNLESS THEY... THEY WOULDN'T...!

SHLAK
HOPE THIS WORKS. ACCELERATOR SET TO *MAXIMUM.*

MAXIMUM THRUST!
EVERYBODY *HOLD ON TO SOMETHING!*

TTENTION ALL COMPLEX
AFF! *MAG STRUCTURAL*
TEGRITY COMPROMISED.
COLLAPSE IMMINENT.
BOSS, I DON'T UNDERSTAND...

THE ACCELERATOR ON THE COMPLEX FLOOR HOLDS AN OPPOSITE CHARGE TO THE DISSIPATOR ON THE CEILING...
SO?

THIS STRUCTURE CAN'T MAINTAIN BOTH LOADS AT PEAK. THEY'RE LITERALLY GOING TO ***TEAR THE ROOF*** OFF THIS PLACE!

SUB LEVEL 1.
ACCELERATION REACHING CRITICAL MASS, SAFETY PROTOCOLS ENGAGING IN 5...4...
HERE GOES...

3...
SLIV, DISABLE SAFETY PROTOCOLS!
ON IT.

2...
SAFETY PROTOCOLS DISABLED.

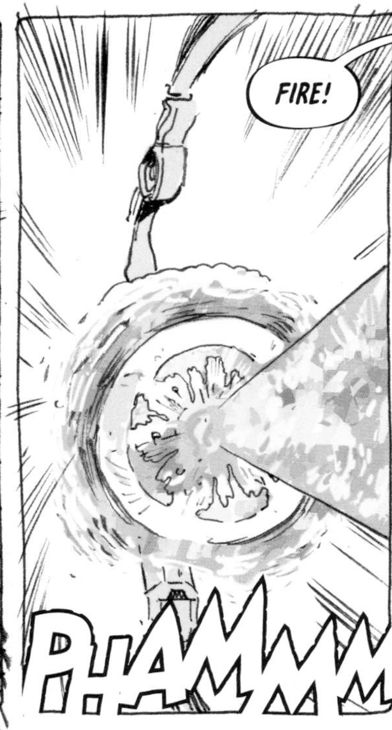
FIRE!
PHAMMM

TARTARUS.
KRAKABOO
HERAKLE
BAR & LOUNGE

I CAN'T BELIEVE IT...
UNNN...

IT WORKED!

ALL PRISONERS. STAY WHERE YOU ARE.
WHAT THE HELL IS THAT--?!

GOOD. NOW, SAY "CHEESE"!

OPEN FIRE!
PHAMM
PHAM
PHAMMM

RUN!

C'MON...STEP ASIDE...

IS THAT KLEEPH?!

HE'S BEEN DUCKING ME FOR DAYS.

KLEEPH! *HEY!*

I SWEAR THAT BASTARD HEARD ME.

THE ESCAPE ATTEMPT.

THEY GOT US PINNED DOWN! LET'S PRAY THE GUNS ON THESE MAGs STILL WORK.

ONLY ONE WAY TO FIND OUT!
I'LL GET YOU A CLEAR SHOT. DON'T WASTE IT.
THERE SHE IS!
PHAMM
PHAMM

C'MON, HELP ME MOVE THIS THING. GET READY TO FIRE.
SCRRUUNCCCH

RRRRRAAAAHHH!

PHOOM

HA! GUESS IT STILL WORKS!

SURKA! COME *ON,* LET'S GO!
GRRRAAH!

SURKA!
POLICE

YOU MADE IT!

THE KEY TO MY HEART.

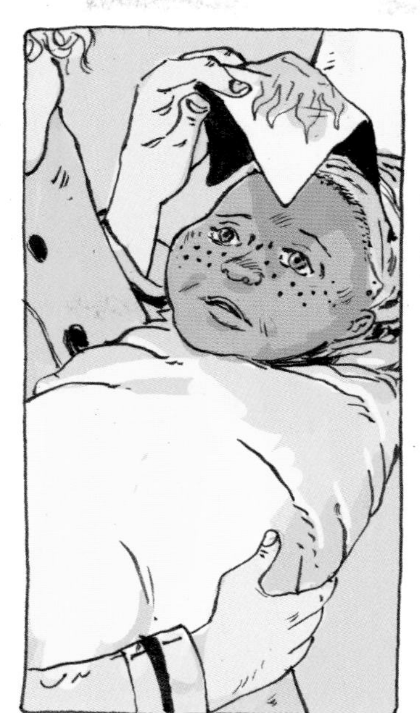

MY DARLING TILDE.

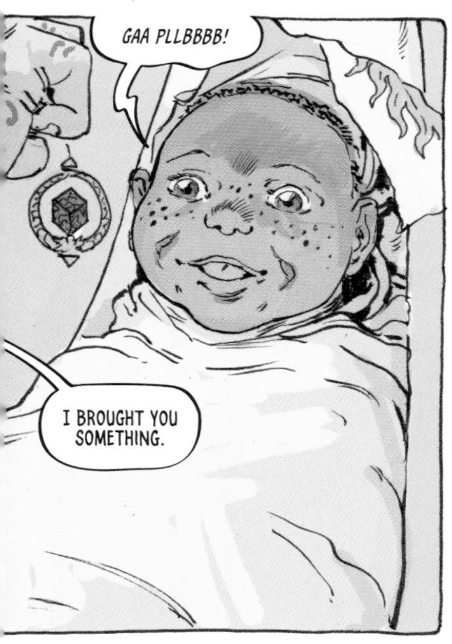
GAA PLLBBBB!
I BROUGHT YOU SOMETHING.

ON A NEARBY ROOFTOP.
GET ME A CLEAR SHOT! I WANT SURKA *DROPPED!*
WHERE ARE THOSE LAST TWO BOZOS?...
I'LL FIND 'EM, SERGEANT KABE.

FIRST TIME WE DITCH GUARD DUTY AND A FREAKIN' *JAILBREAK* HAPPENS!
SARGE'S GONNA HAVE OUR HEADS FOR THIS.
YOUR HEADS ARE WORTHLESS...

FOR A START, THEY'RE *EMPTY.*

IS THAT A *DJINN?*
LET ME HANDLE THIS. I'LL BE RIGHT UP. GO ON, IT'S OKAY

WHAT IS IT, KLEEPH?
REMEMBER *THIS* MOMENT. THIS IS GOING TO BE THE BEST DAY OF YOUR LIFE, GLOH.
IT'S PRIVATE *PREMIERE* GLOH TO YOU.

YOUR NAME IS WHAT I *SAY* IT IS, *"GLOH."* DON'T THINK I WON'T GUT YOU IN FRONT OF YOUR FANCY NEW FRIENDS.
WHA...WHAT DO YOU WANT?

I WANT YOU TO *SUCCEED.* AREN'T YOU TIRED OF BEING A JOKE?
I CAN'T *AFFORD* YO KIND OF *HELP,* KLEE

THOSE REGULATION FLICKERS ARE WORTHLESS AT THIS DISTANCE AND YOU KNOW IT.
BUT *THIS* HERE WILL GET THE JOB DONE. KILL SURKA AND YOU'LL BE A *HERO.*
I THOUGHT SURKA WAS ON *YOUR* SIDE?

SURKA'S A WALKING GENOCIDE. GENOCIDE IS BAD FOR BUSINESS.
AND YOU GET TO *STAY* BOSS.

WIN, WIN, RIGHT?

SURKA!

I, MASTER OF LOCKS, HISA IKEDA, ORDER YOU TO SURRENDER. RESIST AT YOUR OWN PERIL.

I'LL BE RIGHT BACK, TILDE. MOMMY HAS ONE LAST FOOL TO KILL.
SMOOCH

ALIVE OR DEAD...

I'M PUTTING YOU BACK IN THE GROUND.

OOOF!

HA!

WELL...
THUD

THAT WAS PATHETIC.

YOU TRYIN' TO PROVE SOMETHING?
KEEP TALKING.

THE ACADEMY HAS AN ENTIRE CLASS ON HOW TO DEAL WITH YOU...

AND I TEACH IT.

UNNF!

WHAM

GRRAAAH!

DAMMIT, IKEDA IS IN THE WAY!
EVERYONE HOLD YOUR FIRE!
MEANWHILE, TAKE DOWN ANY DJINN REINFORCEMENTS THAT--
SLUG
PRIVATE GLOH, WHAT THE *HELL* DO YOU THINK--
WHRRRR
POP
YOU WANT MY FREED YOU'LL HAVE TO TAK IKEDA. AND NO ON TAKES WHAT'S MIN
PRIVATE! PUT THAT GODDAMNED FLICKER CANNON DOWN, THAT'S AN *ORDER!*
I CAN MAKE THE SHOT, SARGE!
GLUUNG
SHRAAK
NOO!

BOOM
SURKA!
HOOOLY--

CORPORAL...
MY GODS...!

I WANT YOU TO ARREST PRIVATE GLOH...
IT WASN'T... I DIDN'T THINK--!

"FOR THE MURDER OF MASTER OF LOCKS, IKEDA."

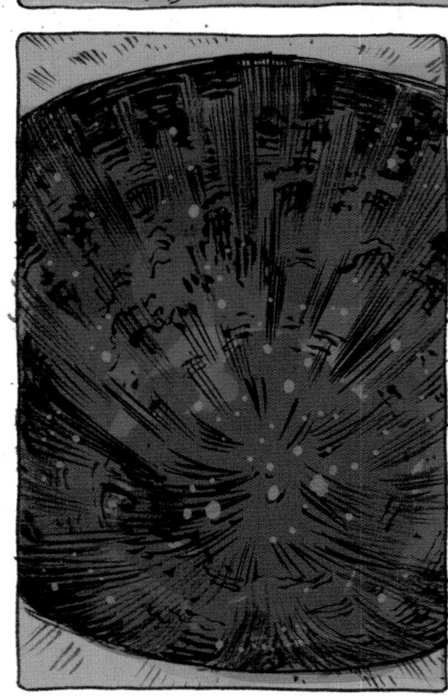

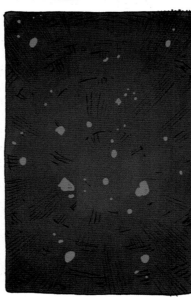

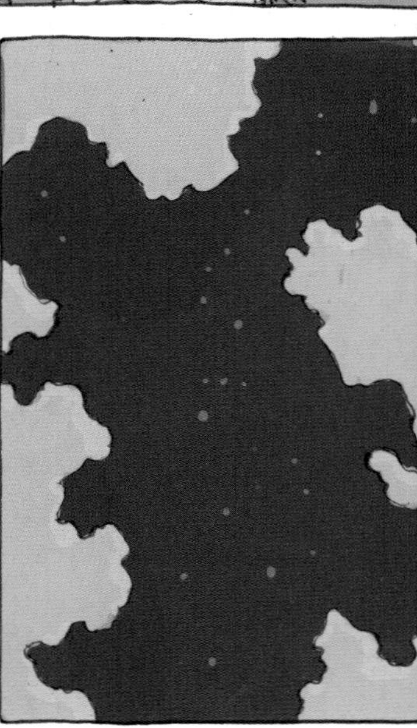

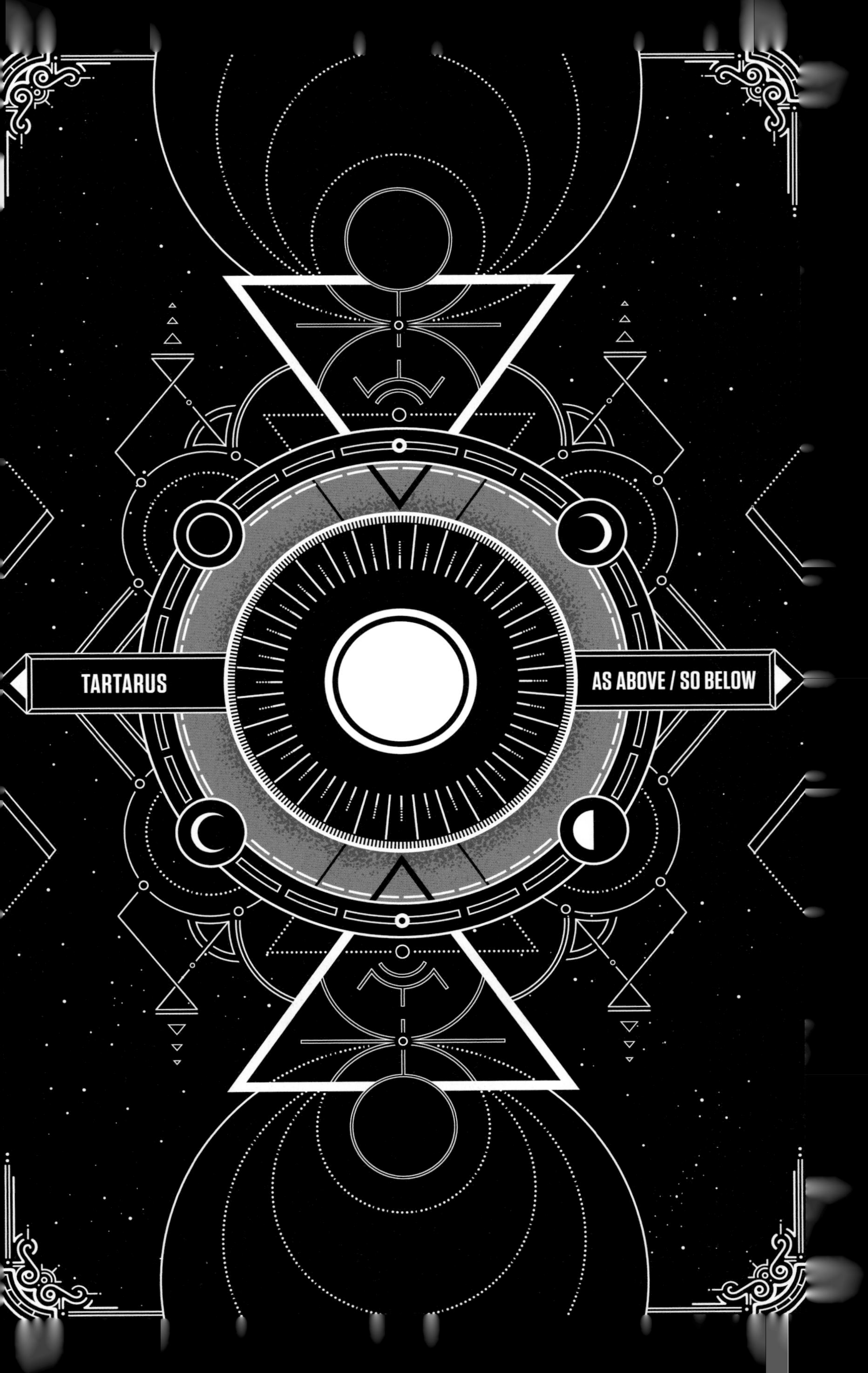
TARTARUS
AS ABOVE / SO BELOW

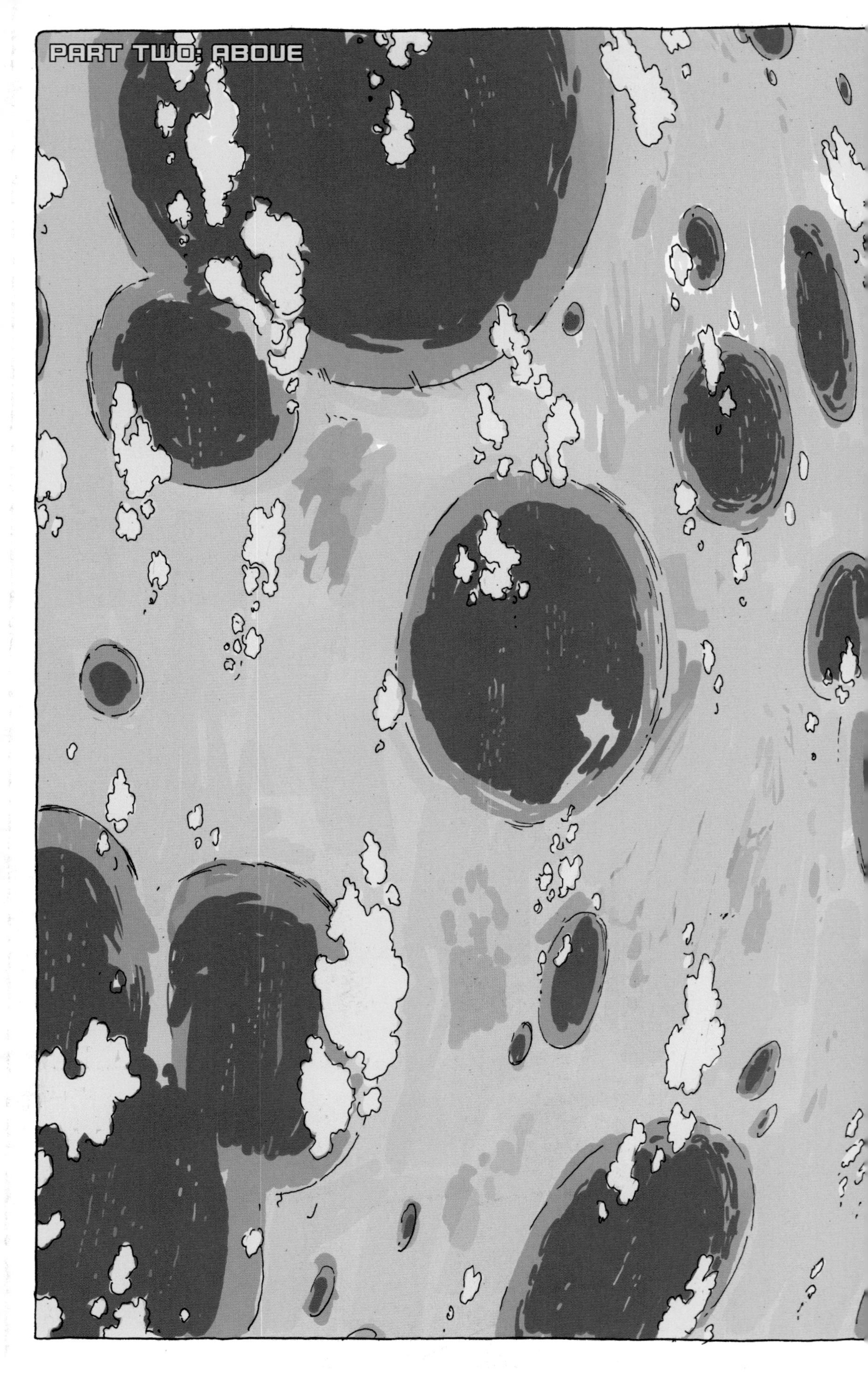
PART TWO: ABOVE

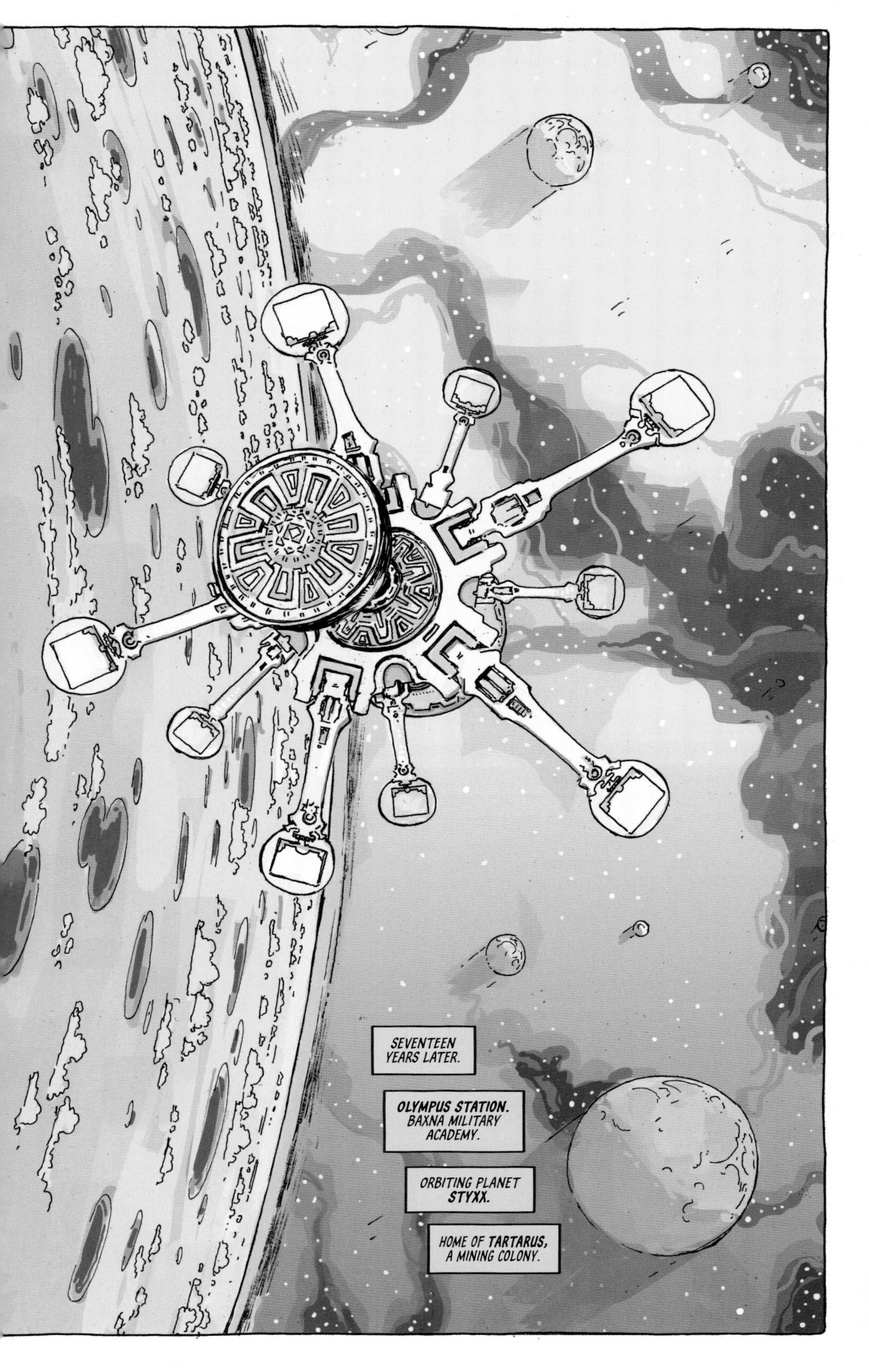
SEVENTEEN YEARS LATER.
OLYMPUS STATION. BAXNA MILITARY ACADEMY.
ORBITING PLANET STYXX.
HOME OF TARTARUS, A MINING COLONY.

BAXNAN MILITARY CADETS ON R&R.
IT'S A MATCH!
STAR CROSSED
QUICK, CALL THE DOCTOR...!
'CAUSE I'M ABOUT TO BREAK ANOTHER HEART!
MINI COMMISSARY
HOW'S THAT, ROMEO?
KLINZU
DESIGNATE: WARRIOR
LUSTY
OSKAN
DESIGNATE: INTEL
BUSY BODY
TILDE
DESIGNATE: ADMI
FARM GIRL
SHE'S ON TARTARUS, KLINZU. WE'RE NOT SUPPOSED TO GO THERE.
0.202.4105
SEE ON MAP
SO?
"SO"? REMEMBER TINTIK?
TINTIK, THE CADET WHO GOT HIMSELF KIDNAPPED DOWN THERE?
OLYMPUS STATION. MOON DECK.
MILITARY WOULDN'T PAY THE RANSOM, SO THE TARTARANS BLEW HIS FACE OFF.
THEY SENT BACK PIECES OF HIM FOR SIX MONTHS. HIS MOM PAID THE RANSOM JUST TO MAKE THEM STOP!
TARTARUS, MURDER & MAYHEM MAGAZINE'S "MOST TANTALIZING HELL HOLE."
THAT'S NOT A REAL MAGAZINE.
WHAT THE HELL'S THE POINT OF "SHORE LEAVE" IF WE CAN'T LEAVE?
YOU WEREN'T KIDDING, SHE IS GOOD LOOKING!

HOW YOU GONNA GET AROUND STATION CHIEF ILZN?
IT'S *HIS* ORDER THAT WE STAY PUT.

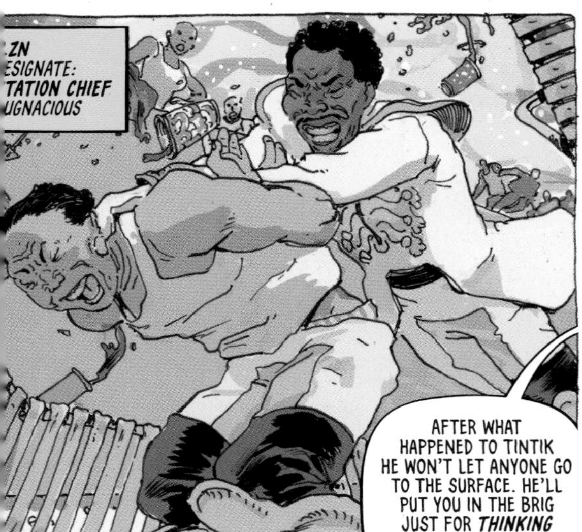
ZN
ESIGNATE:
TATION CHIEF
UGNACIOUS
AFTER WHAT HAPPENED TO TINTIK HE WON'T LET ANYONE GO TO THE SURFACE. HE'LL PUT YOU IN THE BRIG JUST FOR *THINKING* ABOUT IT.

THAT OVERFED HALL MONITOR DON'T SCARE ME.
CHIRP
CHIRP
CHIRP
INCOMING...

RUSH. SLIDE US TO DECK B.
DAMN... ANOTHER GENERAL WAS ASSASSINATED!
PROBABLY GENERAL POZZ. THEY *WARNED* HIM, BUT HE NEVER LISTENS...
DOOT
WHAT MAKES YOU THINK IT'S POZZ? THE ALERT DOESN'T SAY WHO.

BEING GENERAL KABE'S SECRETARY HAS ITS PERKS...
YOU'VE BEEN PEEKING AT HIS INTEL AGAIN, HAVEN'T YOU?
RUSH TRANSPORT, DESCENDING.
IF HE FINDS OUT, YOU'LL FACE THE FIRING SQUAD.

HOPEFULLY IT'LL BE A PUBLIC EXECUTION!
HAR HAR.
I'M SO *JEALOUS* YOU SHIP OUT TOMORR TILDE. I'D GIVE ANYTH TO GET AWAY FROM T COMEDIAN.

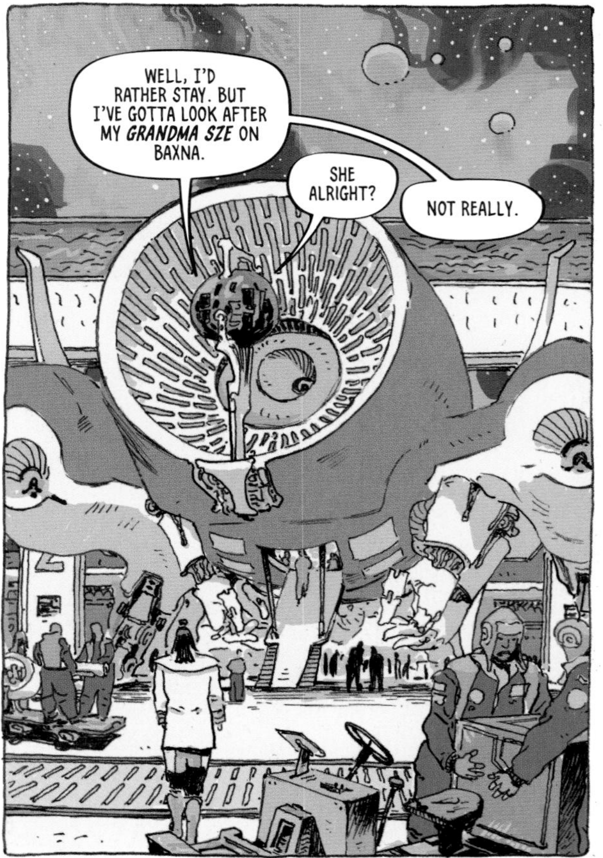
WELL, I'D RATHER STAY. BUT I'VE GOTTA LOOK AFTER MY *GRANDMA SZE* ON BAXNA.
SHE ALRIGHT?
NOT REALLY.

HER RESPIRATORY SYSTEM'S *FALLING APART.* KLETH'S SYNDROME.
SHE LIVE UNDER A ROCK OR SOMETHING? THERE'S A *CURE* FOR KLETH'S.

SHE DOESN'T TRUST DOCTORS, HOSPITALS OR THE GOVERNMENT. SHE WON'T EVEN HAVE FOOD DELIVERED.
SHE RAISED ME SO FAR *OFF THE GRID,* JOINING THE BAXN MILITARY WAS THE ONLY WAY SEE THE WORLDS. AND IT BRO HER HEART...
AH, I SEE...SHE'S A...*MORON.*

EXCUSE ME?!
OR DO YOU PREFER "BACKWARD HAYSEED"? LET'S SWING BY MEDLAB. THEY'LL REPLICATE HER SOME LUNGS. CASE CLOSED.
HA HA HA!

YOU HAVE ARRIVED AT B DECK.
DING
THERE'S NO WAY SHE'S GIVING THE MILITARY A SAMPLE OF--
SHE WON'T HAVE TO, BUMPKIN. SHE'S YOUR GRANDMA. YOU CAN GIVE THEM A SAMPLE.

AS MUCH AS I LOVE HEARING YOU TWO FIGHT, I GOTTA GO! THE GENERAL HATES WHEN I'M LATE.

WATCH HOW YOU SPEAK ABOUT DECENT FOLKS, KLINZU.
AH, DON'T GET BENT OUT OF SHAPE.

MEDLAB.
YOU COMING OR WHAT?

GENERAL KABE'S OFFICE.
MORE ANOMALIES ON THE STAR CHARTS TODAY.
DON'T SWEAT IT. THOSE READINGS ALWAYS GET WONKY BEFORE THE LONG MOON.

DELIVERY FOR GENERAL KABE.
JUST LEAVE IT THERE.

I HAVE STRICT INSTRUCTIONS TO *HAND DELIVER* THIS TO THE GENERAL--
GENERAL'S *BUSY*. I'LL MAKE SURE HE GETS IT.

I'D RATHER--

THAT'LL BE ALL! THANK YOU!

UUUGH...WHAT'S WRONG WITH SOME PEOPLE?

EDLAB.
STRANGE...
YOUR GRANDMOTHER'S RECORDS *APPEAR* NORMAL ON THE CIVILIAN DATABASE...

BUT *OUR* SYSTEM'S NETTING TONS OF RED FLAGS. IF I DIDN'T KNOW BETTER, I WOULD SAY HER RECORDS WERE... FALSIFIED...

YOU MEAN *"INCOMPLETE."* SHE WAS BORN ON AN OFF-WORLD FARM. HER *"RECORDS"* WERE PROBABLY HAND-SCRAWLED ON THE SIDE OF A TUMTUM BARREL.

NO...I MEANT *"FALSIFIED."*
THERE'S SOMETHING ELSE.

CROSS-REFERENCING BOTH YOUR BIO SIGNATURES AND...SHE'S...*UH*...SHE'S *NOT* YOUR GRANDMOTHER. YOU'RE ACTUALLY NOT AT ALL RELATED!

LIQUID ENGINEERING LABS.
SEVNO! WHERE YOU AT?!

STOP FARTING AROUND WITH DJINN TEMPLE REPLICAS FOR A SEC.
I NEED SERIOUS HELP.
YOU CAN SAY THAT AGAIN.

STILL DOING THE DJINN "VOW OF SILENCE" THING TOO, I SEE. YOU'RE OBSESSED!
SEVNO
DESIGNATE: LIQUID ENGINEER
GO-GETTER
I WANT TO BE GOOD AT MY JOB.
THE DJINN ARE THE BEST LIQUID SHAPERS. I WANNA LEARN HOW THEY DO IT.

THE WAY I WAS BEFORE... LOST IN A CARNAL WORLD. THAT WAS OBSESSION.

WHATEVER YOU SAY, BUDDY.
SPEAKING OF CARNAL OBSESSIONS...

CUTE, HUH?
WE MATCHED ON STAR/CROSSED AND--
AND YOU'RE SCHEMING TO GO AWOL...

WAIT...HOW'D YOU HEAR ABOUT THAT?
IF OSKAN KNOWS, THE WHOLE STATION KNOWS. LET'S TALK OVER THERE...
GODS, I PRAY WE STILL DO PUBLIC EXECUTIONS.
WELL, I WANT TO ASK YOU ABOUT YOUR... CONTACT.
C'MON MAN, I KNOW YOU'VE BEEN TO TARTARUS. YOU CAN'T KNOW ALL THIS STUFF ABOUT THE PLACE FROM "RESEARCH."
TARTARUS ISN'T SOME PLAYGROUND FOR HOOK-UPS.

KLINZU, IT'S A DANGEROUS PLACE. PLUS, IF ILZN--
MAN, CHILL--
IF ILZN FINDS OUT, HE'LL RIP YOU IN TWO.

ILZN?! I'M NOT WORRIED ABOUT THAT OVERTURNED GARBAGE TRUCK.

HE'S JUST SALTY TILDE WON'T GIVE HIM THE TIME OF DAY.
WHAT'D YOU JUST SAY ABOUT ME, CADET?

CHECK IT *AGAIN!*

WE'VE CHECKED AND CROSSCHECKED ALL THE PUBLIC DATABASES, TILDE.
YOU'RE SAYING *SZE'S* DOCUMENTS ARE FAKES, AND *MINE* ARE TOO?

YES, ALL FORGERIES.

CHECK AGAINST THE *RESTRICTED* DATABASE.
TILDE, THAT'S NOT SOMETHING I--

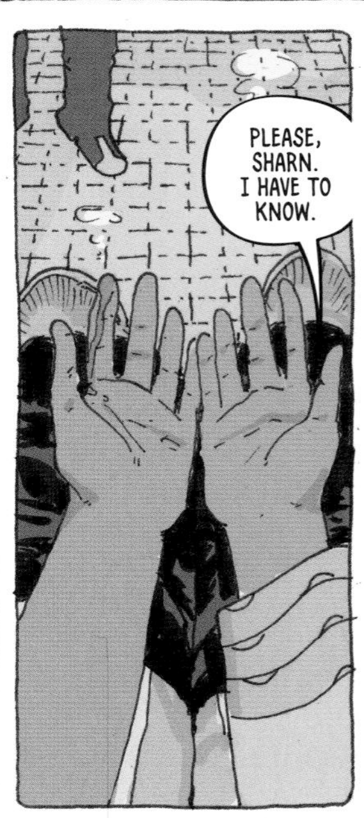
PLEASE, SHARN. I HAVE TO KNOW.

SOON.
OK, WE'RE *IN...* WE'VE GOT ONE HIT. RELATIVE WHO'S BEE
LOCKED UP.

WHAT THE--
ALERT ROOM CONTAINMENT IN EFFECT. ALERT ROOM CON--

ALERT ROOM CONTAINMENT--
SHOOMP

WE'RE LOCKED IN!
WHAT DID YOU DO?!
NOTHING!

SAYS HERE, YOU'VE JUST BEEN FLAGGED AS *SECURITY THREAT!*

NEED TO *RUN.* ***NOW!***
I'M NOT GOING ANYWHERE UNTIL--

CADET HANZA TILDE/348.

COME WITH US.

GENERAL KABE. HIGH COMMANDER OF OLYMPUS.
TEA?

TELL ME CADET, DO YOU LOVE IMPERIUM BAXNA?
YES, SIR. OF COURSE, SIR!

WOULD YOU DIE FOR IT?
THAT GOES WITHOUT SAYING, SIR--
GOOD.

WALK WITH ME.

WHAT DO YOU KNOW ABOUT THE DJINN?
THEY'RE A LIQUID SMUGGLING CARTEL, SIR.
THEY WEREN'T ALWAYS.

THEY STARTED AS *INTERGALACTIC DRILLERS* WHO CAME TO STYXX LOOKING FOR GOLD AND ORE. BUT WHAT THEY FOUND WAS *THE LIQUID.*

THE LIQUID, A SUBSTANCE THAT COULD TAKE *ANY* SHAPE. IT MADE THEM RICH AND MORE PEOPLE CAME. SOON THE DRILLING PLATFORM BECAME A *COLONY.*
WILDCAT COLONIA 27, BUT EVERYONE CALLS IT *TARTARUS.*

A SMALL GROUP OF WORKERS GOT FANATICAL ABOUT *LIQUID SHAPING.* THEY TRAINED MIND AND BODY. MEDITATED, ATE A SPECIAL DIET.
THEY CALLED THEMSELVES *THE DJINN.*
AND BEGAN MAKING THE MOST SOPHISTICATED *LIQUID WEAPONS* IN THE GALAXY.

ROUBLE IS, THEY STARTED *LLING* THOSE WEAPONS TO UR SWORN ENEMIES, THE JURIANS.
THE BAXNAN MILITARY HAD NO CHOICE UT TO STEP IN. WE BLOCKADED TARUS, STOPPING JURIAN ACCESS TO THE LIQUID. TARTARUS'S CRIPPLED ECONOMY WENT DOWN THE TOILET.

TARTARUS, ONCE PROSPEROUS, BECAME A PLACE OF WANT, WAR AND *DEATH.*
THAT'S WHEN THE DJINN TURNED TO *SMUGGLING* AND THINGS GOT *REALLY BAD...*

SIR, WHY ARE--?

WHEN *SURKA* TOOK OVER.

UNDER HER DARK RULE THE DJINN CARRIED OUT A SEASON OF MAYHEM. UNSPEAKABLE ATROCITIES. I WAS THERE, I SAW IT WITH MY OWN *EYES.*

WITH MY OWN *EARS* I HEARD HER WAR DRUMS, MADE FROM THE SKINS OF HER ENEMIES.

PUT THE TEA DOWN.

WHEN WE FINALLY CAUGHT HER, WE CAGED HER IN THE DEEPEST PIT WE COULD FIND.
IN AN ABYSS AT THE FOOT OF THE WORLD. WHERE NOTHING GREW.
BUT IN THAT PIT SHE GAVE BIRTH.

SHE GAVE BIRTH TO *YOU,* TILDE.

I'LL JUST HAVE A LITTLE PEEK.
DEET DEET DWUNG
GREETINGS, KABE, OLD FRIEND. PLEASE DON'T BE ALARMED...

DO YOU LOVE IMPERIUM BAXNA, TILDE?
YES SIR, BUT--
WHEN YOU ENLISTED, YOU PROMISED TO PROTECT BAXNA FROM *ALL* THREATS.

SIR...IT CAN'T BE TRUE.
I'M AFRAID IT IS. STAND *UP,* CADET!

DO YOU KNOW *WHAT* YOU ARE?
*UH...*AN ADMINISTRATIVE ASSISTANT...?
NO, CHILD. AS THE LIVING HEIR OF SURKA, YOU'RE A *THREAT.*

YOU'VE SERVED BAXNA HONORABLY. TAKE MY SWORD, TILDE. YOU'VE EARNED THE PRIVILEGE OF ENDING THE THREAT...
BY ENDING YOUR OWN LIFE.

WE FOUGHT WELL, SARGE.
DID YOU OPEN THAT?
IT... IT...!

THEY'RE COMING FOR US NOW, BUT THEY WILL NEVER...
IT'S A *BOMB!*

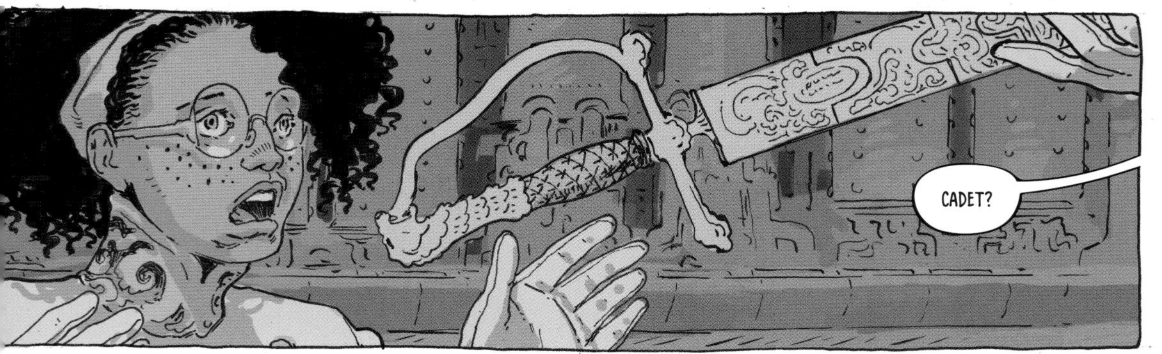
CADET?

YOU HESITATE?

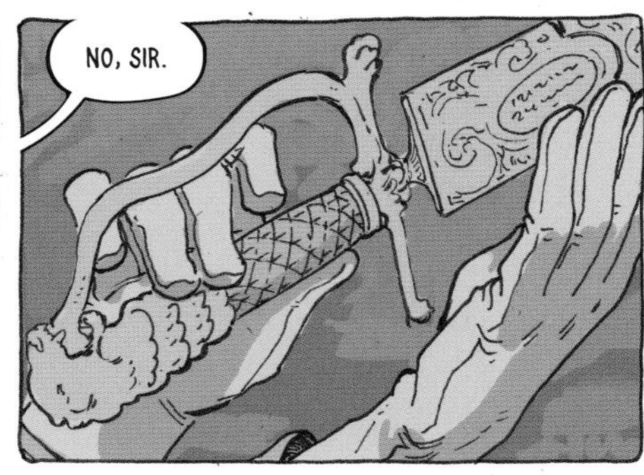
NO, SIR.

BUT YOU'RE *WRONG!*

RUN! IT'S A--
...THE LIGHT!

FWOOOOOM

BOOOM

CRUUUNK

BOOM

FWOOOSH

UHHNNN...
FORM RANKS! I WANT EVERYONE ACCOUNTED FOR AND QUESTIONED.
WE'RE UNDER ATTACK!

BANNED IN BOTH EMPIRES!
PAID ADVERTISEMENT
STAR CROSSED
THE LONG MOON IS COMING
Warm up on the long night with Star Crossed
Imperial Passport®
True intergalactic Dating. Encryption technology circumvents Imperial blocks. Now reach available singles throughout the Baxnan AND Jurian Empires (Eastern Sector Protectorates Excluded)
New Ghosting Feature
Eradicate ghosting and ghosters. Removes offenders from the app, as well as the visible light spectrum for 28 days.
STAR CROSSED
EHZTES LAYCEE /194
ARMS SPECIALIST
TARTARUS
SEE ON MAP
Health Chek
Hacked Imperial medical records display the virility of matching singles.
Matrimony Roulette
New instantaneous Match n' Marry® feature.
Cupid's Arrow
Focused subconscious advertising to your intended. Malevolently Irresistible.
Star Crossed It's written in the stars.
MURDER & MAYHEM MAGAZINE

XIII

CHAPTER TWO

TARTARUS
HOMEGOING

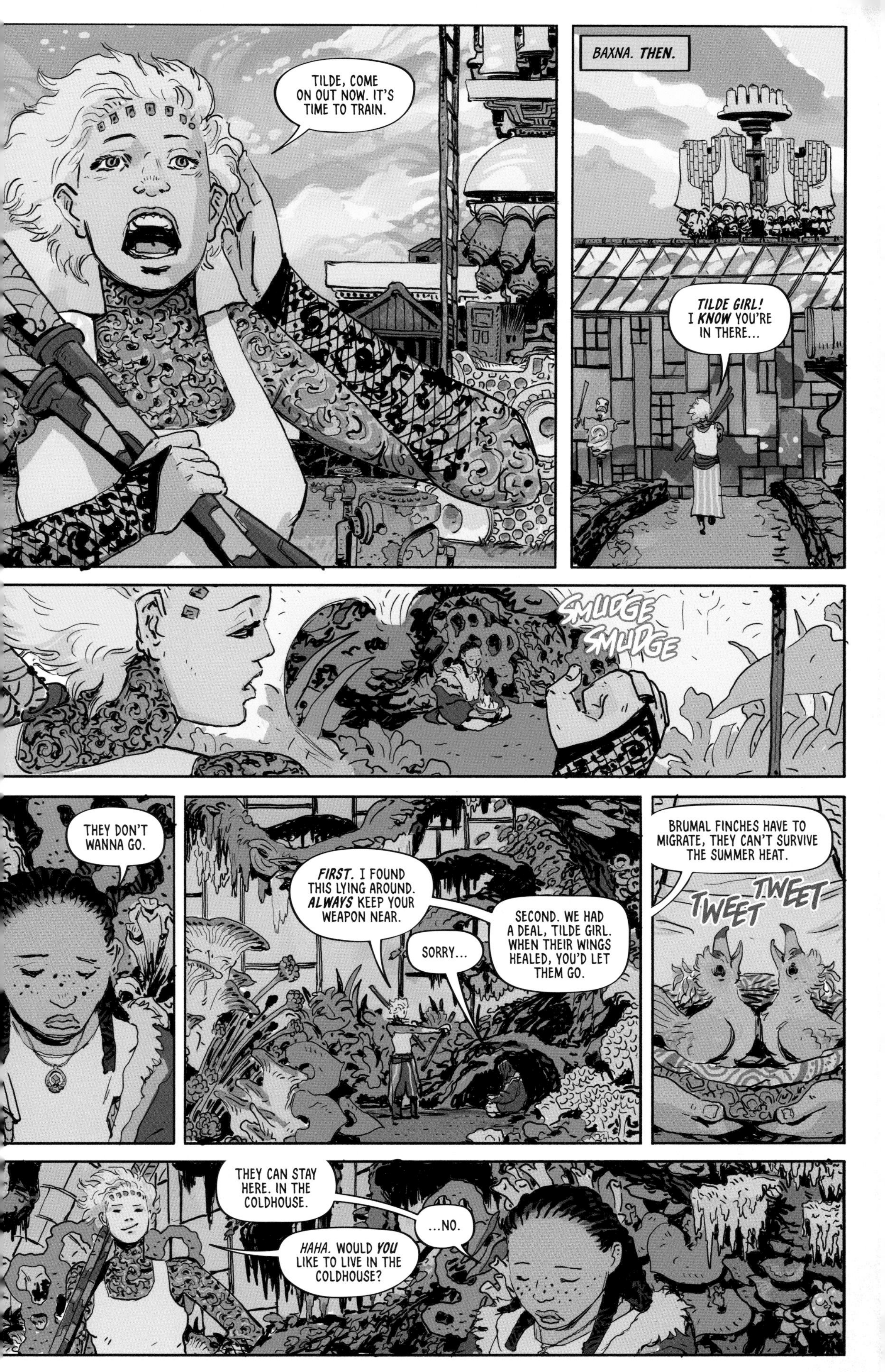
TILDE, COME ON OUT NOW. IT'S TIME TO TRAIN.
BAXNA. THEN.
TILDE GIRL! I KNOW YOU'RE IN THERE...
SMUDGE SMUDGE
THEY DON'T WANNA GO.
FIRST. I FOUND THIS LYING AROUND. ALWAYS KEEP YOUR WEAPON NEAR.
SORRY...
SECOND. WE HAD A DEAL, TILDE GIRL. WHEN THEIR WINGS HEALED, YOU'D LET THEM GO.
BRUMAL FINCHES HAVE TO MIGRATE, THEY CAN'T SURVIVE THE SUMMER HEAT.
TWEET TWEET
THEY CAN STAY HERE. IN THE COLDHOUSE.
...NO.
HAHA. WOULD YOU LIKE TO LIVE IN THE COLDHOUSE?

IF YOU WERE LOST, WHAT WOULD YOU DO?
I'D COME BACK HERE.
WHY?

BECAUSE IT'S MY HOME.
EXACTLY! THESE LITTLE GUYS HAVE A HOME, TOO.

A *REAL* HOME. C'MON, LET'S TAKE 'EM TO THE BLUFFS.

NEXT WINTER, THEY'LL BE BACK! YOU'LL SEE. ALL GROWN UP. WITH GREAT BIG COLORFUL FEATHERS!
COLORS?!
LIKE A RAINBOW!

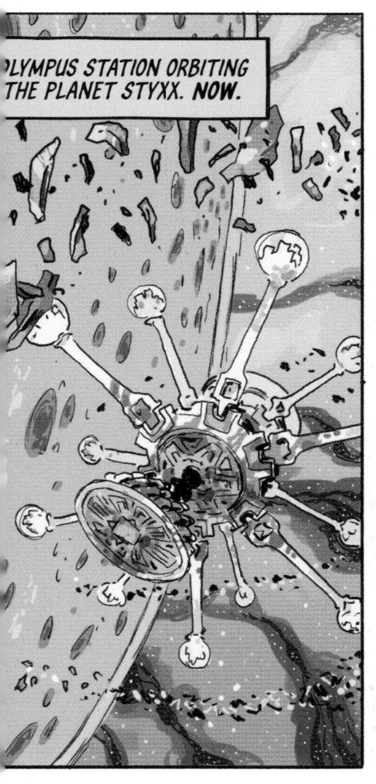
LYMPUS STATION ORBITING THE PLANET STYXX. **NOW.**

JURIA CLAIMS THEY'VE GOT NOTHING TO DO WITH THIS.
LYING BASTARDS.

, THREE BAXNAN ERALS HAVE BEEN DERED IN THE LAST SIX MONTHS.
TELL ME SOMETHING I ***DON'T*** KNOW, CORPORAL, SUCH AS, WHERE'S GENERAL KABE?

NOTHING ON THAT YET, SIR, BUT...IT DOESN'T LOOK GOOD. THE EXPLOSION WENT OFF NEAR HIS OFFICE.
THE RAT THAT DID THIS LIKELY WENT UP IN FLAMES, TOO.

OR IS TRYIN' TO SCAMPER FREE. SCORCHED TAIL BETWEEN THEIR LEGS.
Hanza Tilde/348

SOMEBODY'S GONNA PAY FOR THIS.

PRIORITY ONE: LOCK DOWN OLYMPUS...

"I DON'T WANT ANYONE COMING IN OR GOING OUT."
DEEP IN THE BOWELS OF OLYMPUS STATION.

GOING SOMEWHERE, KLINZU?
HUH...?! WHA...?! COURSE NOT!

EVEN YOU WOULDN'T TRY TO SKIP OUT DURING A STATION LOCKDOWN, WOULD YA, KLINZU?
TILDE...! YOU GOT IT ALL WRONG, THIS ONLY LOOKS--

LOOKS LIKE YOU'RE ABANDONING THE STATION DURING AN EMERGENCY TO GO ON A STAR/CROSSED DATE!
LOOK, TILDE...DON'T SQUEAL ON ME...I...I CAN PAY YOU...I'VE GOT SOME EXTRA DRACHMAS--
SAVE IT, KLINZU. YOUR MONEY AND YOUR EXCUSES.
ONLY THING I WANNA KNOW ABOUT YOUR LITTLE JOYRIDE...

...IS IF THERE'S ROOM FOR ONE MORE?

WHERE WERE YOU BEFORE THE ATTACK?!
AAARRGGHH!
WHERE?!
BOSS! WE GOT A LEAD.

WELL...?
IT...IT WAS TILDE, SIR.

WATCH YOUR STINKING MOUTH, CORPORAL!
JOR, YOU GONNA BACK ME UP HERE?!

SHE'S FROM A DJINN FAMILY, SIR, BIOLOGICAL TESTS CONFIRM. SHE WAS TAKEN TO GENERAL KABE FOR QUESTIONING.
YOU'RE WRONG. TILDE WOULDN'T DO *THIS.*

SHE'S THE LAST PERSON SEEN WITH KABE, BEFORE THE EXPLOSION. IF SHE SURVIVED, SHE'S LIKELY TRYING TO GET OFF THE STATION AS WE SPEAK.

I'LL LOOK INTO THIS *MYSELF.*
INADVISABLE, SIR. THE SUBJECT IS DANGEROUS AND LIKELY ARMED.
ARMED?
KABE'S SWORD IS MISSING.

UNBELIEVABLE.
I'M DOING THIS *ALONE.* AND GODS HELP YOU IF YOU'RE WRONG, CORPORAL.

LIQUID ENGINEERING LAB.
NO.
IT WAS RISKY JUST GETTING SPOTS FOR US, KLINZU.
SEVNO, JUST HEAR ME OUT--

KLINZU IS A HORNBALL. I GET WHY HE WANTS TO GO. WHY DO YOU WANT TO?
HEY!
WHY DO YOU WANT TO?

I GOT THE CONNECT, I ASK THE QUESTIONS.
SHE NEEDS TO GET BACK TO BAXNA. CAN'T WAIT FOR THE LOCKDOWN TO LIFT.

IS THAT WHAT SHE TOLD YOU?

LOOK, I JUST W
SOME ANSWER

DON'T WE ALL...?

THERE ARE NO "ANSWERS" IN THE MOUTH OF HELL. ONLY VERY SHARP TEETH.
AND THAT'S **WHERE** WE'RE HEADED: TO **TARTARUS,** NOT BAXNA.

YOU TELL HER WE'RE GOING TO TARTARUS?
I JUST NEED ***OFF*** THIS STATION, I'LL MAKE MY OWN WAY TO BAXNA.

HEH HEH, CUTE.
YOU'RE ALREADY SMUGGLING ***THIS*** BOZO, WHAT'S ONE MORE?
GUYS, I CAN HEAR YOU!

FINE, IT'S YOUR LIFE.
BLACKMAIL MIGHT WORK ON KLINZU, BUT KHARS IS GONNA WANT **MONEY.**

KHARS! ***THAT*** LUNATIC IS THE SMUGGLER?!
LOTS OF MONEY.

COME ON... THERE'S ONLY ONE TRANSPORT OUT AND IT LEAVES **TONIGHT.**

STAY CLOSE.
PSSST...I'M ALMOST GLAD YOU'RE COMING.

TARTARUS IS SUPPOSED TO BE SERIOUSLY MESSED UP!
I HEAR THEY GOT THREE-LEGGED HORSE-LIKE THINGS DOWN THERE. THEY'RE TWELVE FEET TALL, CARNIVOROUS AND GOOD PETS!

HALF THEIR HUMAN POPULATION IS DEAD ON ARRIVAL. 'CAUSE EVERY BIRTH'S A TWIN BIRTH. ONE ALIVE, THE OTHER STILLBORN.
FIRST KID TAKES ONE LOOK AROUND AND SAYS, "...NAH."

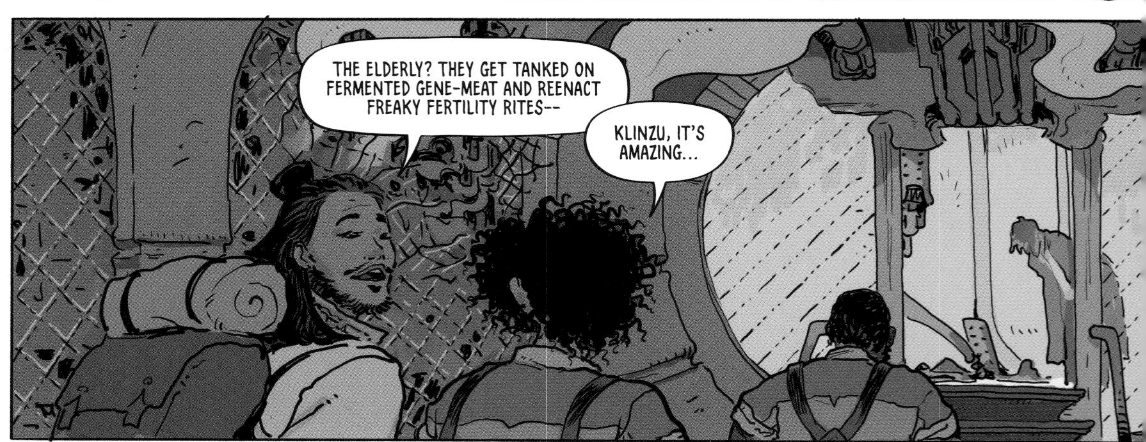
THE ELDERLY? THEY GET TANKED ON FERMENTED GENE-MEAT AND REENACT FREAKY FERTILITY RITES--
KLINZU, IT'S AMAZING...

EVERYTHING YOU JUST SAID.
WAS PROFOUNDLY STUPID.
GUYS, LOOK ALIVE...

OUR RIDE IS HERE.
KHARS
DESIGNATE: DEATH FERRY CAPTAIN
SMUGGLER

OOM
BOOM
ARANS ARE SUPERSTITIOUS.
A BE BURIED ON TARTARUS
N FORTY-EIGHT HOURS OF
ATH. THAT'S THE CUSTOM.
EARS BACK, A CONTRACT WORKER
ED UP HERE AND WASN'T FERRIED
BACK FOR THREE DAYS. THEIR
WORKERS' UNION WENT ON
STRIKE FOR A MONTH.
TOILETS WERE BACKED UP THROUGH C DECK. EVER SINCE, IF THERE'S A DEAD TARTARAN HERE, WE MAKE SURE THEY GET HOME. PROMPTLY. EVEN DURING A TOTAL STATION LOCKDOWN.
BOOM
BOOM
AND THERE'S A LOT OF DEAD ONES TODAY...LIMITED ROOM. SO MY SERVICES ARE GONNA COST YOU DOUBLE.
DON'T LOOK AT ME! MY DRACHMAS ARE FOR A VERY FANCY DINNER WITH AN AWFULLY LUCKY LADY.
BOOM
BOOM
WILL THIS COVER IT?
YEAH. THAT'LL DO.
WELCOME.

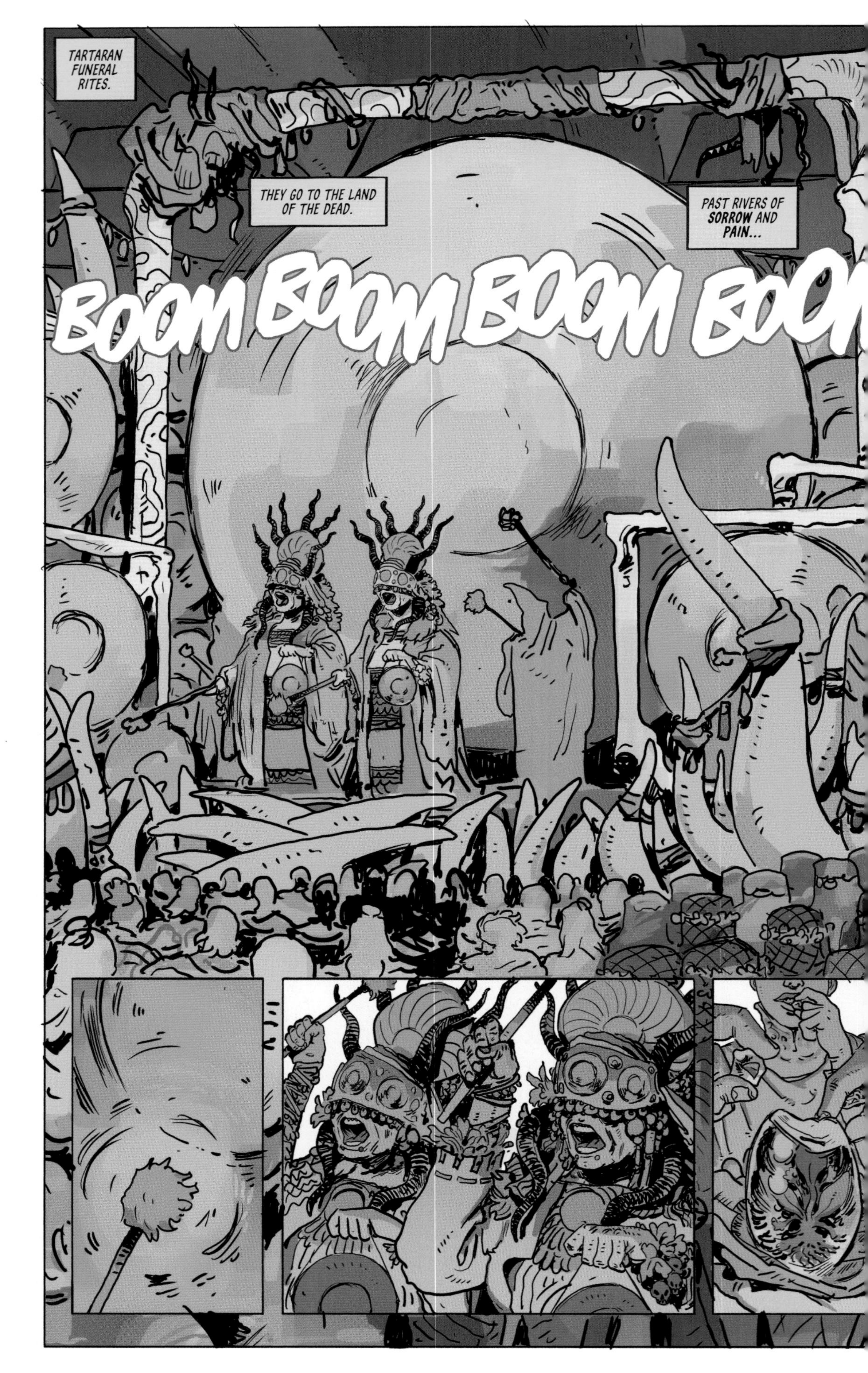
TARTARAN FUNERAL RITES.
THEY GO TO THE LAND OF THE DEAD.
PAST RIVERS OF SORROW AND PAIN...
BOOM BOOM BOOM BOO

OF FIRE AND OBLIVION.
SOULS, FREE FROM RAPTURE OR WAILING RETURN...
HOME.
TARTARAN RETURN TRANSPORT AKA THE FERRY

THE FERRY'S CARGO HOLD.
GET IN. THERE'S A SARCOPHAGUS FOR EACH OF YOU.
EAT THIS. IT'LL PUT YOU TO SLEEP AND SLOW YOUR HEART RATE **WAY** DOWN. YOU'LL BE JUST ANOTHER STIFF TO STATION SCANNERS.
THIS STUFF WORKS FAST!
TILDE!

GET OUT OF THE BOX AND DO IT SLOWLY.

FLEEING THE STATION AFTER AN ATTACK? YOU'RE COMING WITH ME.
ILZN, IT'S NOT--
OLYMPUS COMMAND, DO YOU READ?
⸗KSSSHH⸗

AS FOR THE REST OF YOU CLOWNS, IT'S DERELICTION, AT THE VERY *LEAST*. AT WORST, *TREASON*.
⸗KSSHH⸗ THIS IS OLYMPUS COMMAND. WHAT ARE YOUR ORDERS, CHIEF ILZN?

CRACK

DAMMIT. THROW THIS BUSYBODY OUT THE AIRLOCK.

KHARS! WAIT, DON'T KILL HIM...!

I'LL PAY YOU TRIPL--⸗
FIRE UP THOSE ENGINES! LET'S GET A MOVE ON BEFORE MORE COMPANY SHOWS UP.

TARTARAN RETURN TRANSPORT. REQUESTING DEPARTURE, OLYMPUS STATION.
DEPARTURE GRANTED. SAFE RETURN.

AYE. TARTARAN RETURN TRANSPORT. BEGINNING DESCENT.

≶GASP≶
TWEET TWEET

THANK THE GODS!...JUST A DREAM.
TWEET TWEET

TWEET TWEET

TILDE! I *KNOW* YOU'RE IN THERE...
TWEET TWEET

IF YOU WERE LOST, WHAT WOULD YOU DO?

COME HOME!
6814
TWEET TWEET TWEET

GASP!

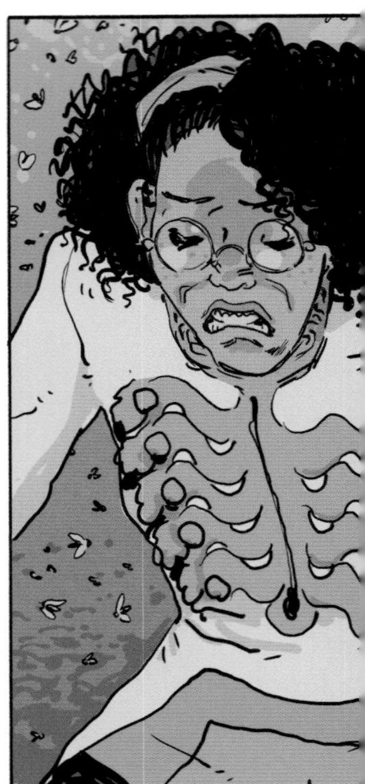

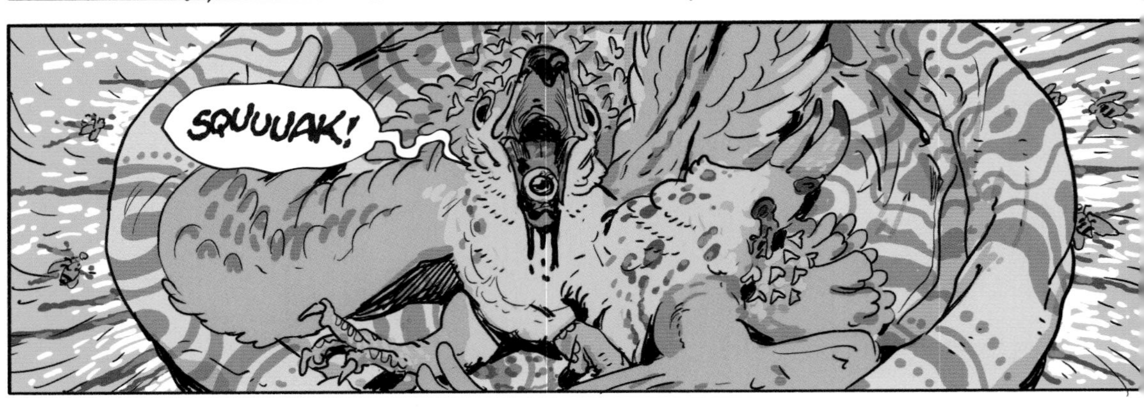
SQUUUAK!

GASP!

PANT!
PANT!

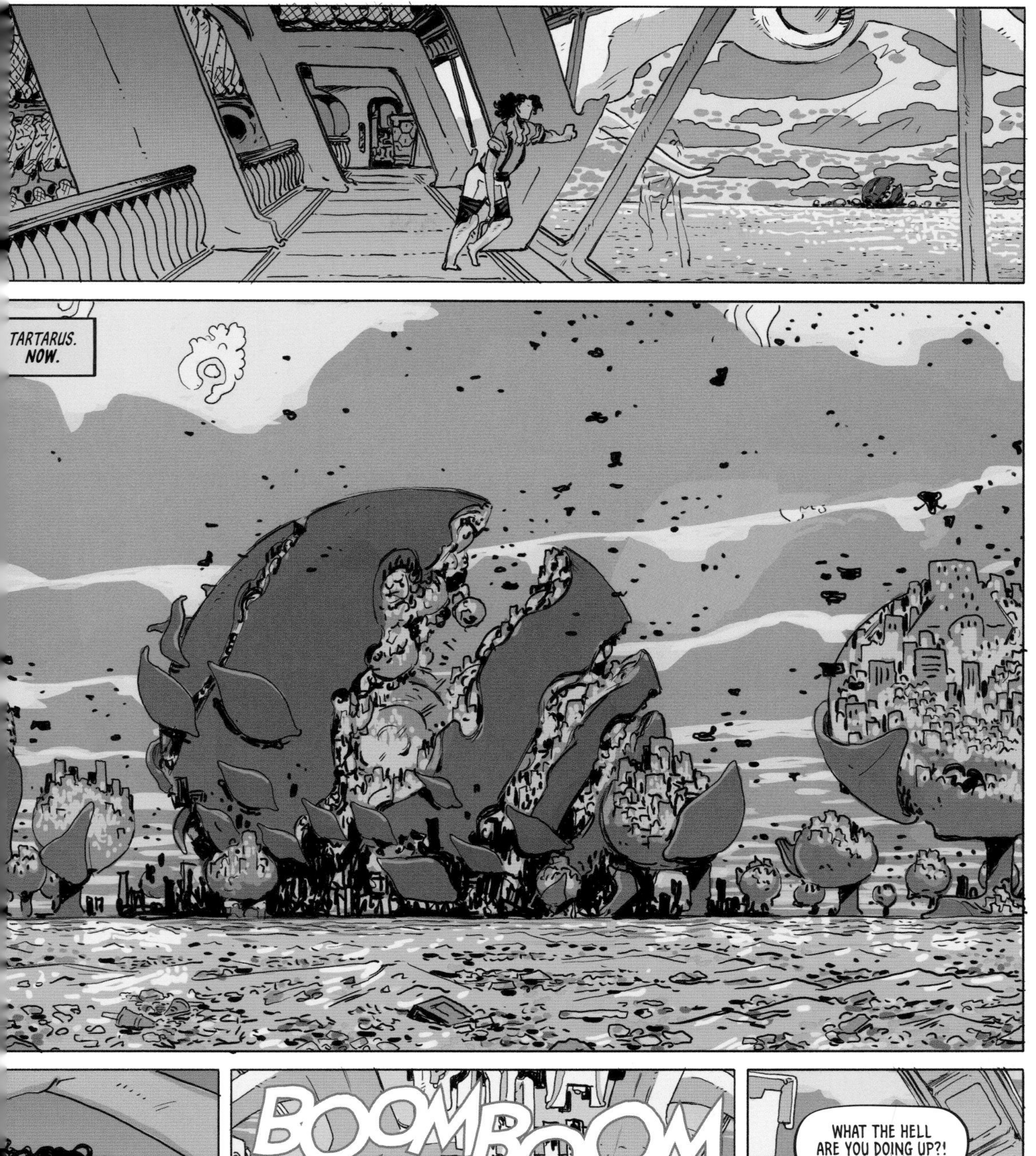
TARTARUS.
NOW.

IT'S BEAUTIFUL...

BOOM BOOM
MORE LIFT ON STARBOARD!
WE'RE TOO HEAVY, CAPTAIN!

WHAT THE HELL ARE YOU DOING UP?! STRAP IN!
INITIATING EVASIVE MANEUVERS!

WE'RE UNDER ATTACK!
BOOM

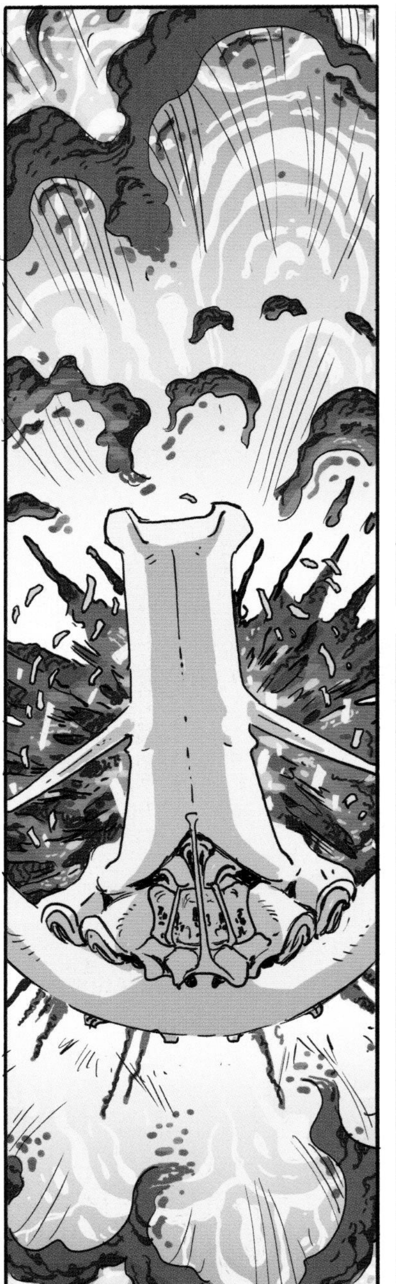

UNGHH! WHY WOULD ANYONE ATTACK A FUNERAL FERRY?!
EVERYBODY HOLD ON TO SOMETHING!

WE'RE COMING IN HOT!

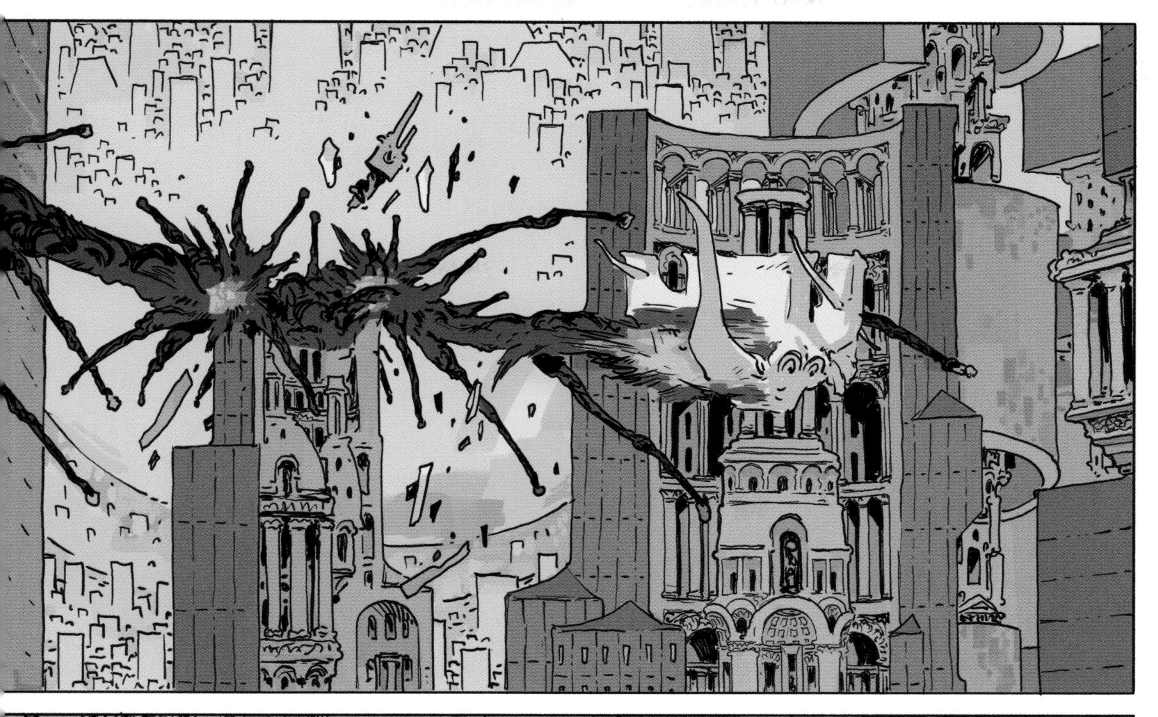

TIME TO GO TO WORK.

WE'RE ON *FIRE!*
SEVNO, IF YOU CAN HEAR ME BACK THERE, SHELTER IN PLACE. EVERYONE ELSE, *BRACE!*

FWAAM

CRON

RUN!

WHERE'S SEVNO?!

THEY'LL BE DEAD IN MINUTES AND SO WILL *YOU* IF YOU DON'T SCRAM. I'LL HOLD THESE GUYS OFF.
FWING
FWING
PHWEEM
PHWEEM

PHWEEM
BUT...
I *SAID*, **GET LOST!**

KLINZU!

KLINZU! LET'S GO!

WE'RE NOT GONNA DIE HERE!

C'MON...

IMPERIAL BAXNAN MILITARY

REQUEST ORDER

Re: Application to Open Internal Investigation

Code 3409: *Suspicion of smuggling*

SUBJECT OF PROPOSED INQUIRY

HANZA KHARS/6

(Name)

CAPTAIN *(Provisional)*

(Grade)

(Signature)

(Fingerprint)

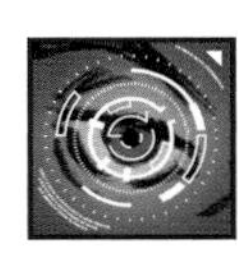

(Retinal scan)

RECORD AND SERVICE

- ▲ Officer training Baxnan Military Academy
- ▼ Conviction on grounds of illegal organ transport
- ▼ **Sentenced**: 11 Lunar Cycles of incarceration
- ▼ **Served**: 48 Lunar Cycles of incarceration *(due to repeated infractions)*
- ▲ Reinstated in Defense Ring
- ▲ Reclassified, re-certified in Mortuary Transport

CLASSIFICATIONS/CERTIFICATES

- Mortuary Transport
- Low Atmosphere Vehicle certification: *Theta Class*
- Time at current rank: CAPTAIN (in poor standing) / four years
- Accident Report: ████████
- Accidents that caused bodily injury or dismemberment: ████████████████████
- Applied Certificate in Tartaran Morturary Rites
- Applied Certificate in Baxnan Mortuary Rites
- Justice of the Peace

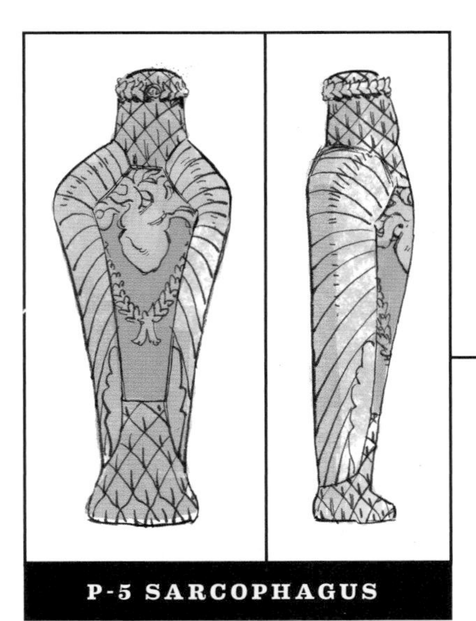

P-5 SARCOPHAGUS

Certification in P-5 SARCOPHAGUS Technology
Repair, refrigeration and maintenance of P-5 Sarcophagus.

PERSONAL DATA/MISCELLANEOUS INFO

- ▲ Marital Tradition: Dark Void Polyamory
- ▼ Marital Status(es) Respectively: DIVORCED, SEPARATED, COMPLICATED, MISSING *Status Unknown*
- ▼ Known descendants: 19 *(Disputed, all. Paternity claims pending.)*

XVI

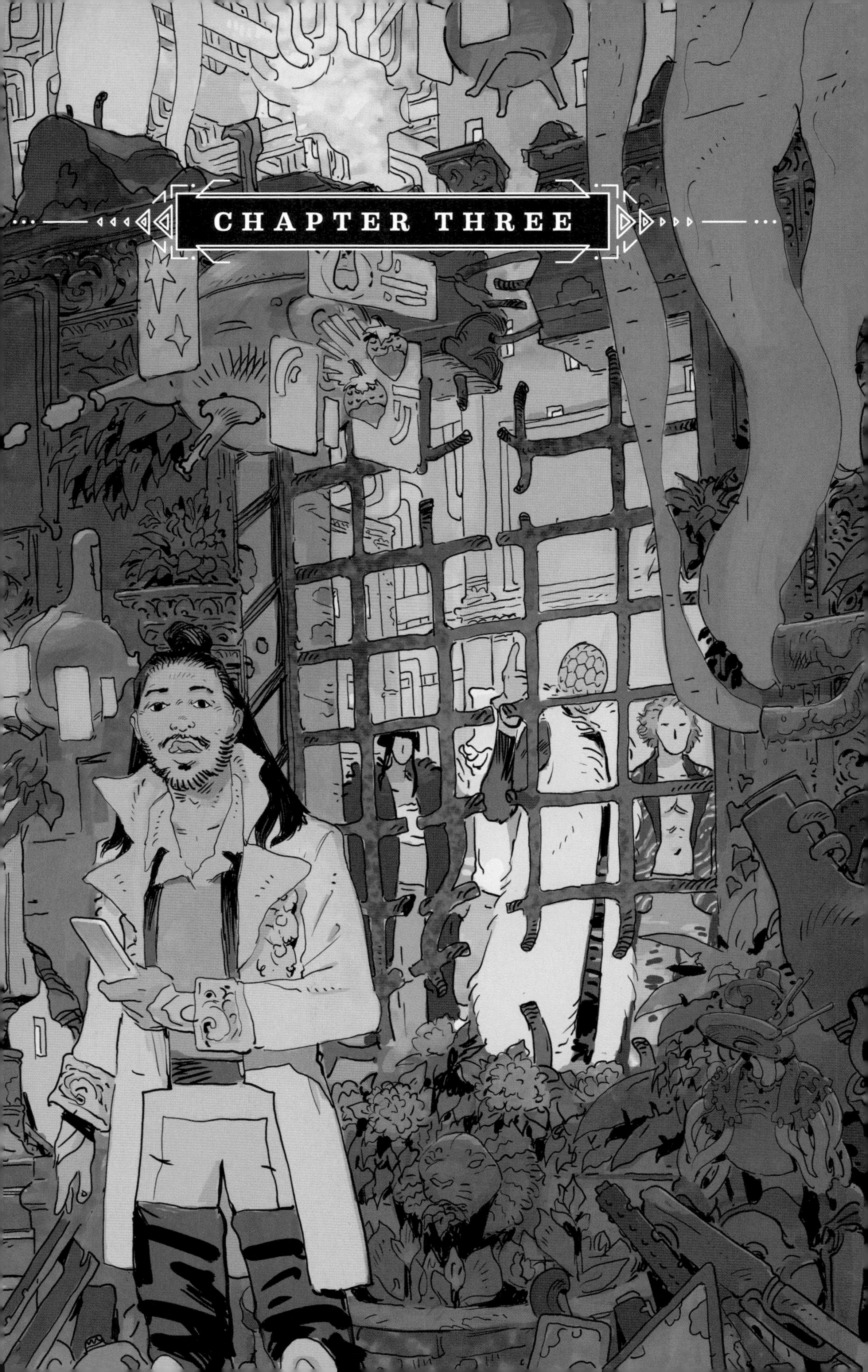
CHAPTER THREE

TARTARUS
LOVE X SQUALOR

TARUS.
DEADLY MINING COLONY ON
N OCEAN PLANETOID AT THE
ASS-END OF SPACE.
IF MIDNIGHT WORE A CROWN, TARTARUS WOULD BE THE BLACK PEARL AT THE CENTER OF IT. DEATH HERE IS MORE COMMON THAN LIFE.
PHWEEM
GAH!
PHWEEM
ING
FWING
FWING
DAMN VULTURES!
THIS IS KHARS. MOST AT HOME BETWEEN LIFE AND DEATH, HE'S SAILED INTO THIS PORT A THOUSAND TIMES.
PHWEEM
FWING
SOON AS I GET TO THAT MOUNTED GUN, IT'S GAME OVER FOR YER ASSES.
PHWEEM
S SMUGGLING CONNECTIONS ARE MY TICKET TO BAXNA.
THERE'S A BARGAIN TO BE HAD, A DEAL TO BE STRUCK,
HARS HAS CAJOLED HIS WAY TO THE BETTER END OF IT.
THESE NEW LIGHT RIFLES AIN'T WORTH A DAMN!
RELOAD... RELOAD, DAMMIT!
CLONG
I SWEAR, IF I GOTTA KEEP DEALING WITH THIS LOW-GRADE CRAP, MY HEAD'S GONNA--!
HE'S NEVER LEFT HOLDING THE DIRTY END OF THE--

OH NO.
PHWEEM
THAT WAS N
SUPPOSED T
HAPPEN...

CHECK THE WRECKAGE FOR VALUABLES. AND KEEP YOUR EYES OPEN FOR THE *ASSET.*

GOOD CALL, TILDE.
WHAT?!
OVE
THE

GET THEM!

DEAR CUSTOMERS, THE MARKET IS NOW CLOSED. DISEMBARK IN AN ORDERLY FASHION.
IT WAS *YOUR* IDEA TO LEAVE HIM!

THAT WAS *HIS* IDEA!
MY IDEA WAS TO DRAG *YOUR* ASS TO SAFETY.
FOR THE **FINEST** FASHIONS, FIRST-RATE SYNTHETIC ORGANS...

VINTAGE SCANTRON SHEET MUSIC, THE BEST DEALS IN RAYMOZ DISTRICT...
DAMMIT, TOO LATE. IT'S CLOSING TIME.

WILL BE HERE AGAIN SOON!
PHOOM
PHOOM
PHOOM

GODS. YOU ARE SUCH A *DI--*
WHOA!

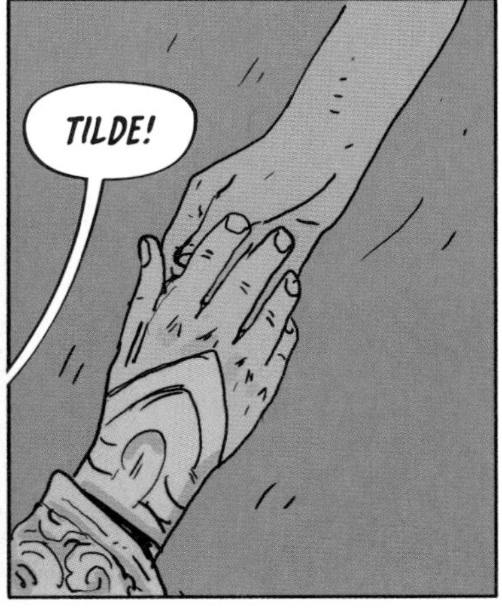
TILDE!

DON'T LEAVE ME HERE!
THE MARKET'S HEADING TO JUKO STATION, WE CAN STILL GET THERE BEFORE--
NEVER MIND HER.

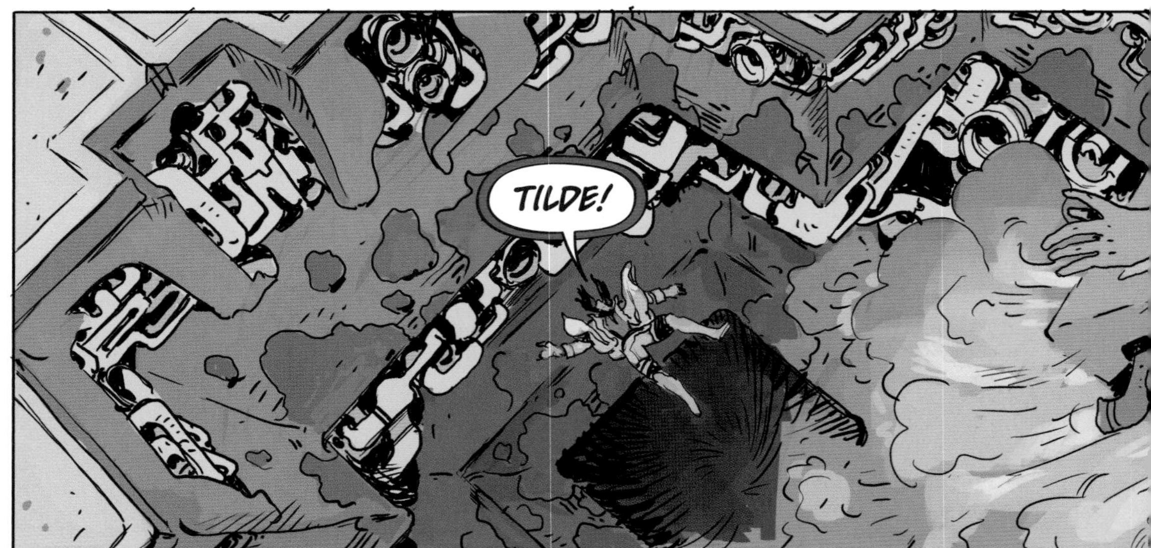
TILDE!

HE'S THE ONE WE WANT.

FIND ANYTHING USEFUL?
ONLY THIS *KICK-ASS* SWORD...

AND A BOX OF--
GIMME THAT.

WHAT THE...?
BOSS?

IMPOSSIBLE...!
WHAT IS IT?

WHAT ARE YOU WAITING FOR?! BRING ME THAT BUFFOON. I'LL CATCH UP.

FIRST, I GOTTA CHECK SOMETHING OUT.
UNFF...

PING
YOUR MATCH IS NEARBY!

I'VE GOT TO FIND MY OWN WAY MY HOME NOW, MY OWN SMUGGLERS.
THIS BUNCH LOOKS PROMISING...
...HE RAN OFF. GOT A DRILLING GIG ON WILDCAT 103.
I TOLD YOU HE'S A SCUMBAG.
HAPPY
WHY DIDN'T SZE TELL ME? WAS IT FEAR?
FEAR OF THIS PLACE, WHERE THE AIR SMELLS LIKE CARDAMOM AND ISOBUTYLENE. TASTES LIKE OVERRIPE MANGOES AND MAGNET SHAVINGS.
DISCERNING PATRONS OF JUKO DISTRICT!
THAT'S BIG TIME BUCKS, BOY, PLUS HAZARD PAY. YOU'RE JUST JEALOUS HE GOT IT, NOT YOU.
STILL DON'T MAKE IT RIGHT.
GATHER 'ROUND FOR DEALS ON DEALS!
HOW WE GONNA FIND A NEW CREWMAN IN FOURTEEN HOURS?
WE'RE SCREWED.
UNSETTLING HOW UN-ALIEN THIS PLACE IS.
ASTRAL WHALE BONE POWDER FOR THE AMOROUS, NUYU® DESIGNER GENE KITS FOR THE EXPECTING...
OK. THEY'RE DEFINITE UP TO SOMETHING.
WAS SMUGGLING TO BAXNA ALWAYS THIS HARD?
JACKPOT!

FOR
LORD-GOVERNOR
OF TARTARUS
GLOH

WATCH IT, CUR!
UNNFF!
BUMP

DRACHMAS, MISTER?
UH...SORRY... I'M...SORRY...

YOU MADE IT!

I MEAN...YOU ACTUALLY CAME?!

I'M CHEYA, YOUR STAR/CROSSED DATE!

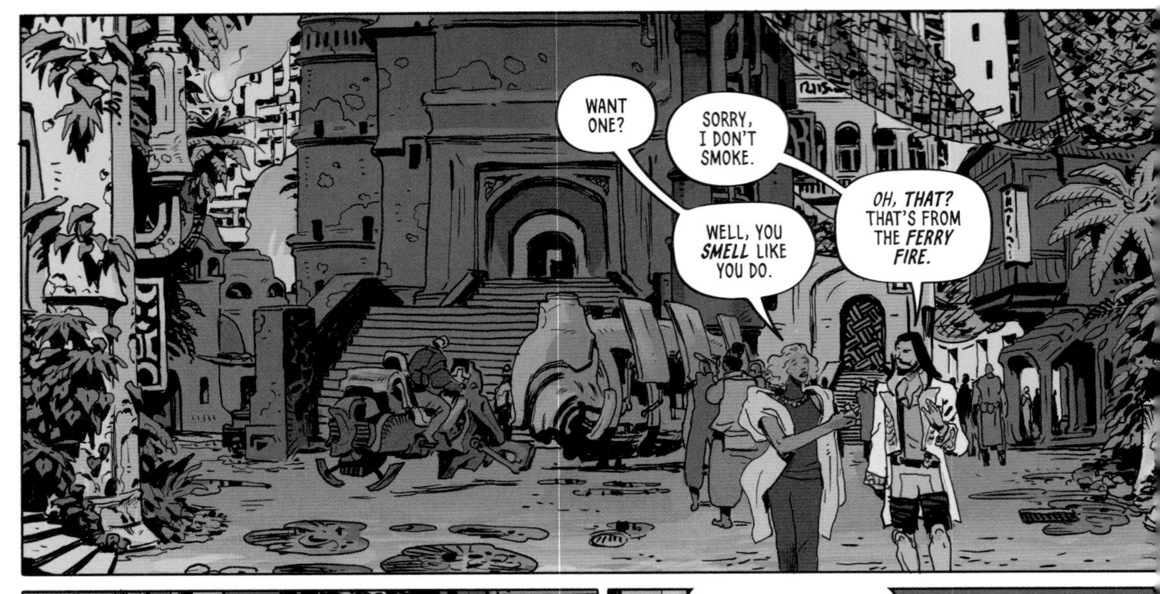
WANT ONE?
SORRY, I DON'T SMOKE.
WELL, YOU *SMELL* LIKE YOU DO.
OH, THAT? THAT'S FROM THE *FERRY FIRE.*

COME AGAIN?!
IT'S A LONG STORY.
SO THIS IS IT, *HUH?* DOESN'T SEEM SO BAD.

I MEAN, I DON'T SEE ANY *BLOODBATHS...*
IF YOU'RE LOOKING FOR ANIMALS, KLINZU, I CAN POINT YOU TO THE ZOO.
BUT THIS IS WHERE *LIVE.*

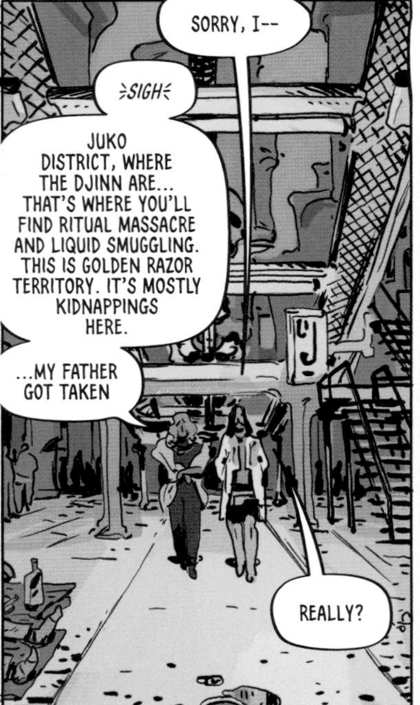
SORRY, I--
SIGH
JUKO DISTRICT, WHERE THE DJINN ARE... THAT'S WHERE YOU'LL FIND RITUAL MASSACRE AND LIQUID SMUGGLING. THIS IS GOLDEN RAZOR TERRITORY. IT'S MOSTLY KIDNAPPINGS HERE.
...MY FATHER GOT TAKEN
REALLY?

REALLY. THE CROOKS THINK WE'RE FLUSH, SINCE OUR FAMILY WAS ONE OF THE FIRST TO SETTLE HERE. BUT OUR PRESTIGE OUTLASTED OUR WEALTH.
DAMN.
YEAH.

WELL...
GROWING UP ON BAXNA MUST BE A LOT DIFFERENT, I BET?
JURIA, ACTUALLY FAMILY O DEFECTED BAXNA A YEARS A

AREN'T JURIA AND BAXNA?...
SWORN ENEMIES? YEAH. DAD SOLD STATE SECRETS TO BAXNA FOR A SMALL FORTUNE AND SAFE PASSAGE.
HOT-PEPPER

AND THE BAXNANS ACCEPTED YOU?
WHO NEEDS ACCEPTANCE WHEN YOU'VE GOT A TRUST FUND?

HAHAHA!
HEH. WHAT?

BESIDES, FEELING LIKE AN OUTSIDER KEEPS ME ON MY TOES.
I GET IT. YOU'RE ***STRONG,*** YOU DON'T NEED ***ANYONE.***

RY STRONG! TAKE OK AT THAT QUAD, FINEST SPECIMEN IN THREE STAR SYSTEMS!
THAT'S NOT THE STRENGTH I MEANT--

WATCH ME PUT THESE MONEYMAKERS TO WORK. GONNA WIN YOU A BOATLOAD OF PRIZES! WE'RE GONNA NEED A ***GURNEY*** TO DRAG 'EM OUT OF HERE.
LEG POWE

SOON.
THOSE MACHINES ARE RIGGED...
AWW, I LIKE MY LITTLE POOKIE PRIZE.

HEY, CHEYA... ABOUT YOUR DAD, THE RANSOM...I CAN HELP. MY FAMILY MAY BE SHORT ON HONOR, BUT WE'RE LONG ON RESOURCES.

UH...

THAT'S PROBABLY NOT VERY ROMANTIC...
KLINZU, THA COMPLETEL *SELFLESS.*

DOES THAT BREAK A CURSE OR SOMETHING? ARE YOU GONNA TURN INTO A PRINCE?

ALRIGHT, ALRIGHT!
HEY, SERIOUSLY. THAT'S VERY SWEET, THANK YOU. BUT I'M WORKING ON IT, DON'T WORRY, REALLY.

ANYWAY, THIS IS ME.

WANNA *COME IN* TELL ME ABOUT T FERRY FIRE?

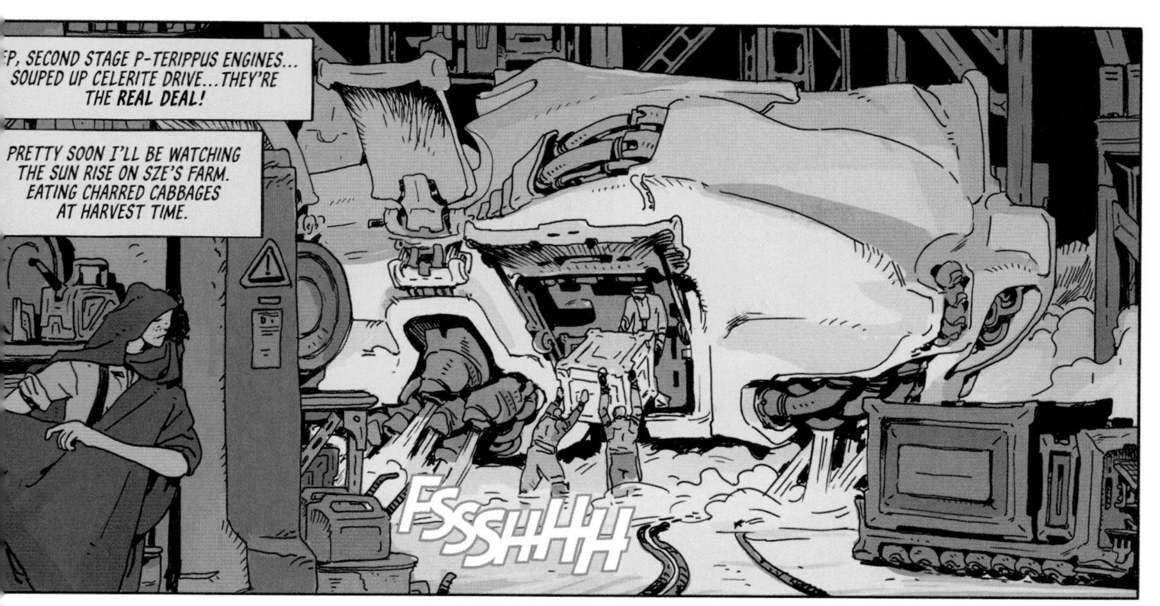
EP, SECOND STAGE P-TERIPPUS ENGINES... SOUPED UP CELERITE DRIVE...THEY'RE THE **REAL DEAL!**
PRETTY SOON I'LL BE WATCHING THE SUN RISE ON SZE'S FARM. EATING CHARRED CABBAGES AT HARVEST TIME.
FSSSHHHH

HIS **NIGHTMARE** EHIND ME, I'LL EVER THINK OF HIS PLACE AG--

DON'T LEAVE ME HERE!

IT'S A MATCH!
STAR CROSSE

SIGH.
0.202.4105
SEE ON MAP

DAMN YOU, KLINZU.

OUCH!
BITE

I'M REALLY SORRY...
HEH, DON'T WORRY ABOUT IT.

SHE AIN'T APOLOGIZIN' ABOUT YOUR LIP, GENIUS!

PUCKER UP!

HE ORACLE'S TEMPLE. DJINN TERRITORY.
HE'S BRAVE COMING HERE.
HE'S ONLY BRAVE IF YOUR BACK IS TURNED.
JIRM, WHEN I SHOOT YOU...

IT'LL BE RIGHT IN YOUR BIG UGLY FACE.
BOYS! SHHHPP

EAR BOY! RARELY COME O SEE ME NYMORE.
COME IN, THE LONG MOON IS ALMOST HERE!
APOLOGIES, SUN. I CAN'T STAY. HOPING YOU CAN ELP ME SOLVE A RIDDLE...
A RIDDLE?

WHERE'D YOU FIND THAT?

NO HARM MUST COME TO HER! YOU TURNED YOUR BACK ON US, THAT'S YOUR CHOICE. BUT SHE'S OURS!

THANKS TORSUN. I'LL STAY LONGER NEXT TIME, I PROMISE.
SHE'S OURS!

BOSS IS ON HIS WAY.
YOU DONE GOOD, CHEYA.
WHERE'S MY DAD?

A DEAL'S A DEAL. HE WALKS FREE TONIGHT.
THIS WAS PLANNED? A HOSTAGE EXCHANGE?
BEEN PLANNING IT FOR WEEKS, HAVEN'T YA, CHEYA?
FLPAWP

SNARED A BAXNAN SOLDIER FROM A **RICH** JURIAN FAMILY.
WILLING TO VISIT A ***STRANGER,*** ON AN ALIEN WORLD, ***ALONE...*** EASIEST MONEY WE'VE EVER MADE.

DID YOU EVEN LIKE ME AT ALL?
HAHAHA OH, OH, THIS IS ***TOO*** TRAGIC!

LET'S GET OUT OF HERE.
WHERE'D YOU PUT THAT SWORD?
THIS SWORD?

HANDS OFF! THAT CADET BELONGS TO THE BAXNAN DEFENSE RING, OLYMPUS CELESTIAL PHALANX. HE'S QUITE UNBEARABLE. BUT HE'S NOT ALONE.

THREE AGAINST ONE. REMEMBER SZE'S TRAINING...
AAAIIIEE!
FWWOOSSH
EVEN THE ODDS BY ATTACKING ANDROIDS FIRST.

LET HIM GO! FINAL WARNING!
IGNORE THE FEAR...

YOU'RE WARNING US? THAT'S RICH!

CLANG
UHHT.

KSSHHNNG
FINE.

...FEAR, SPROUTING LIKE VINES.
HAVE IT YOUR WAY!
OOOF!
THUDD

LOOK, I DON'T WANT TROUBLE. RELEASE HIM AND WE ALL WALK AWAY!
NAH, YOU'RE STAYING. AFTER I GUT YOU, YOUR CARCASS'LL FETCH A FAIR PRICE AT THE VULTURE PENS.

AAAHHHHGG!
GETTING THE POINT NOW, LITTLE SOLDIER?
FEAR, CRUMPLING MY STOMACH LIKE A SONIC HAMMER...
THIS AIN'T A WAR GAME ON OLYMPUS. YOU'RE WITH US NOW, DOWN IN THE MUD. HERE WE DON'T SWING A SWORD, UNLESS WE'RE READY TO--
GOTCHA.

FEAR OF WHAT I MIGHT BECOME.
AAARRGHH!
SHLSSSHHH

PHWEEM PHWEEM
ENOUG
KRISH

PUT YOUR WEAPON DOWN OR I *WILL* SHOOT.

ICE HER, BOSS.

SHOOT HER!
NO.
THAT'S NOT HOW WE DO THINGS.

YOU KILLED ONE OF OURS. BY GOLDEN RAZOR TRADITION YOU HAVE TWO CHOICES: REPLACE HIM OR DEATH BY--
DEATH.
ZZPP ZZZZP

WHAT?
I'M NOT JOINING YOUR KIDNAP CLUB. JUST GO AHEAD. ***SHOOT.***

FINE.
RRRMMM!
YOU THOUGHT I MEANT YOU? NOOOO, I'M SHOOTING *HIM*.
BOSS, DON'T! THE RANSOM!
KRAK
HELL WITH *THAT!* A CHOICE WAS MADE.
PHWWWW...
WAIT!

OK! I'LL DO IT.

SAY
IT.
LIKE YOU
MEAN
IT.
I'LL REPLACE YOUR FALLEN SOLDIER!

TODAY IS JUST NOT MY DAY.
GREAT!

SORM, TAKE THE ASSET AND GO. I'MA CHAT WITH OUR NEW RECRUIT.

HURK!
TILDE. I'M--
DON'T.

MMMM...
...THE LINE OF ARES.
NO WAY...
THE WAY HOME...
FLLLK
TCH
TCH
TCCCH

WANT ONE?
THIS IS YOURS, RIGHT?
IT BELONGED TO MY *MOTHER.*
OUR MOTHER.

WE HAVEN'T BEEN PROPERLY INTRODUCED.
HI, I'M MOGEN. YOUR TWIN BROTHER.
...WILL BE MUCH TRICKIER THAN I THOUGHT.

0

CHAPTER FOUR

TARTARUS
DOGS OF TARTARUS

IMPORTANT SAFETY WARNING

Your new Jaxsa Stimplant includes a flaring valve to prevent liquid shaping related brain damage.

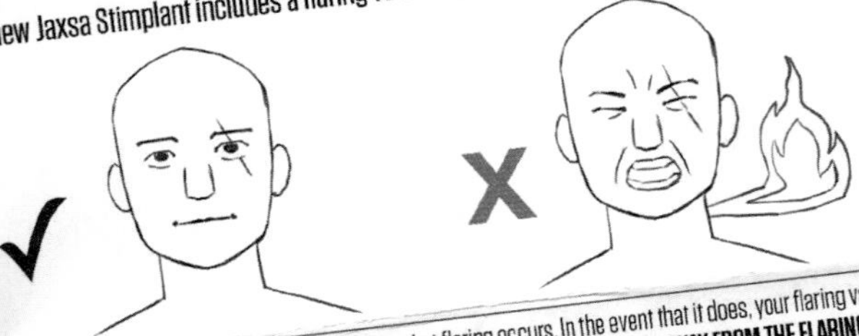

It is best **NOT** to utilize your Stimplant to the degree that flaring occurs. In the event that it does, your flaring valve will release the byproducts of excess use. **KEEP HANDS AND/OR FLAMMABLE OBJECTS AWAY FROM THE FLARING VALVE.**

Jaxsa's Stimplants accepts no responsibility for any injury or property
...lting from the use of your stimplant flaring valve.

Skip years of training with

JAXSA'S STIMPLANTS

WHAT ARE STIMPLANTS?

Stimulation Implants upload your mental blueprint directly into the Liquid, making it easier to build structures or weapons with your mind (informally called *Liquid Shaping*).

HOW ARE WE DIFFERENT FROM TRADITIONAL *LIQUID SHAPING*, AKA "THE DJINN METHOD?"

The Djinn dedicate years of mental and physical training to learn how to embed blueprints into Liquid... but who has time for that? With *Jaxsa's Blueprints*, you'll be shaping Liquid days after you're off the surgical table.

HOW ARE WE DIFFERENT FROM OTHER STIMPLANT PROVIDERS?

With 20 years experience as former battlefield surgeon in the Baxnan/Jurian War, Jaxsa performs every stimplant operation herself *(with a whopping 74% survival rate)*. Our three-week surgical intervention and recovery takes place in an undisclosed location on a secure low-orbit satellite.

IMPROVED FEATURES!

- Robust testing to ensure *Stimplant blueprints work everytime®*
- 80% fidelty translation of mental map to blueprint to Liquid

OPTIONAL WORKSHOPS ON:

- *Liquid Architecture and form*
- *Basic Blueprints*
- *New Flaring Valve, lowering risk of "brain-melt"*

What are you waiting for?
Build the terrifying weapons of your dreams today!

SHAPE LIQUID *like a Dji*

RTARUS. SCENE OF
THE FERRY CRASH.

TRRCH-CRRSH

THUD THUD
MMM MPPFF MMMMMPPFFF!

WRRRRANKKH

RRRRAAAHH!
CADET SEVNO?!

WHERE IN HELL ARE WE?

DEN RAZOR LAIR.
OSTAGE PENS.
G'MORNING. HERE TO CHECK ON KLINZU.
I WON HIM A *MEAL PACK* IN A GAME OF *JURIAN POKER.*
GONE.
PARDON?

HE'S *GONE.* REACHED HIS *EXPIRY* DATE.
THE HELL IS THAT SUPPOSED TO--

THERE WAS NO RESPONSE TO RANSOM DEMANDS...

FIRST WE SEND NOTES, THEN WE SEND PIECES...*OF HIM.*
THEN PIECE AFTER PIECE AFTER *PIECE...*
COOKIE-PIE

TIL WE GET WHAT WE *WANT.*"
MUTILATION CONCOURSE.
YES. YOU'LL LOOK *DIFFERENT* AND IT'LL BE *PAINFUL.*
BUT KEEP THE WHINING DOWN, OK? GETTING TIED UP IN KNOTS ABOUT YOUR OLD SELF-IMAGE IS *SO* UNBECOMING.
ZZZZZTTTT
E GODS
P--!

I CONFESS.
I'M PRETTY ATTACHED TO...BEING *ATTACHED.*

BUT I'M PRETTY GOOD AT NOT GETTING *TIED UP* IN *KNOTS!*

CRACK
REGARDING PAIN AND SELF-IMAGE...

HOPE YOU DON'T MIND ME REARRANGING YOUR *FACE!*
THUD

TAKE 'EM DOWN!

WHAM

ALRIGHT, FUN'S OVER!
SUBDUE THE PRISONERS!
BZZZZT

HUFF
HUFF

UNGS ROOM. GOLDEN
ZOR'S PLANNING AND
STAGING AREA.
HEY, SIS.
MOGEN, YOU HAVE TO STOP THEM!
THEY'RE GOING TO--

NO-CAN-DO, SIS. WE NEED THAT MONEY. BUT DON'T WORRY, HE'LL LIVE.
SYGHUS
LEADER OF THE
GOLDEN RAZOR

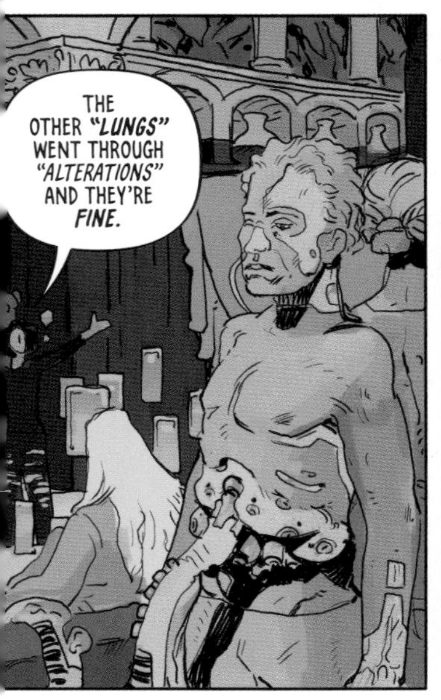
THE OTHER "LUNGS" WENT THROUGH "ALTERATIONS" AND THEY'RE FINE.

BAXNA DOESN'T PAY RANSOMS. YOU KNOW THIS!
IT IS FRUSTRATING. BUT WE'LL NEVER CHANGE THE WORLD IF WE DON'T TRY.

WHEEZE
MOGEN...
SORRY, TILDE, GOTTA GET BACK TO THIS. LUNCH AFTER?
I'LL PAY THE RANSOM!

⋟SNICKER⋞ WITH WHAT?!
⋟WHEEZE⋞
MOGEN. MY PATIENCE...
APOLOGIES, SIR.
TILDE, YOU HAVE TO GO. NOW.
I'M SERIOUS!
SYGHUS, THERE'S A STASH OF BAXNAN DRACHMAS HERE ON TARTARUS!

HOW MUCH?
IT'S A WAR CHEST FROM A LONG AGO CAMPAIGN... ENOUGH FOR THREE HOSTAGES, MAYBE?

"HOSTAGES?" IT'S AN HONOR TO SERVE AS LUNGS FOR SYGHUS, ADEPTUS EXEMPTUS OF THE GOLDEN RAZOR!
WH IS

ONLY AFTER YOU LET KLINZU GO.
HA!
DOES HE LOOK L DIMWIT TO YO
FUNNY, ARE TWI

YOU WERE SAYING BEFORE THE INTERRUPTION?
RIGHT.
THESE AREAS HERE AND HERE. HIGH CONCENTRATION OF TARGETS...

OK.
I'LL SHOW YOU NOW, IF YOU DON'T HURT KLINZU!

IR?
≥WHEEZE≤
MOGEN AND I NEED THE ROOM.

I DON'T TRUST HER!
I'LL KEEP THAT IN MIND, SORM.

I'VE GOT A GOOD FEELING ABOUT THIS.
HAVE FAITH IN SORM'S JUDGEMENT.
≥WHEEZE≤
YOU HAVE A LOT TO LEARN ABOUT MISPLACED TRUST.

NN TEMPLE.
THE PAST.
BRAVO! BRAVO!
≥WHEEZE≤
"I BLAME YOUR CONDITIONING BY THE DJINN...PFFEH!
"MAKING YOU SOFT. FEEDING YOU APPLES FROM A SILVER TROUGH.
"LIKE A PIG TO BE SLAUGHTERED...

"WARNING YOU TO BEWARE THE TITAN...
CRRAASH
"THE GOD-KILLER, GLOH."

SHHHH SHHH...DON'T INTERRUPT THE SHOW!
"BUT WHEN HE STUMBLED INTO VIEW, YOU KNEW THIS WAS NO GOD-KILLER.
"HE WAS ONLY A COWARD, WHO CRAWLED TO INFAMY ON A BELLY SOFTER THAN MILK..."
≥WHEEZE≤
!

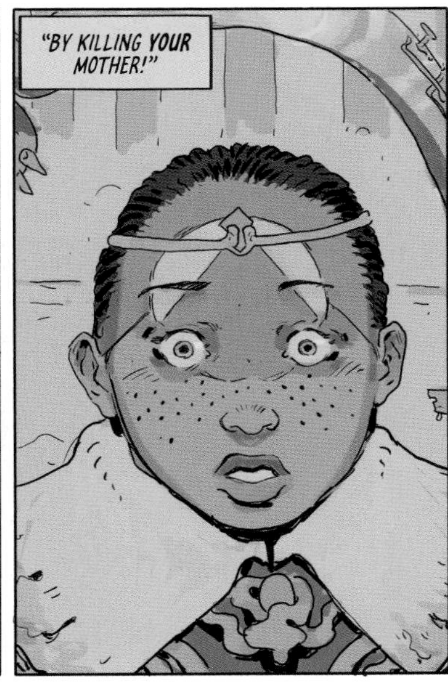

"BY KILLING YOUR MOTHER!"

"BUT THE REAL HEARTBREAK WAS KNOWING THE WORM WOULD NEVER HAVE HAD THE GUTS..."

KEEP HIM OFF OF ME!
HAHAHA!
WHAP

≥WHEEZE≤
"TO RAISE A GU
TO HER...

"UNLESS THE DJINN PUT IT IN HIS HAND."
DON'T BE STUPID.

LORD MOGEN. PLEASE.
FINISH YOUR BEAUTIFUL PLAYING!

"EVEN AS A CHILD YOU KNEW THEY BROKE THE CARDINAL RULE: LOYALTY TO THE DEATH...
"AND TO THE DEATH, LOYALTY."
GGGRRAHHH!
≥WHEEZE≤
"YET HERE YOU ARE AGAIN..."

"MISPLACED TRUST. CALLING TILDE 'SISTER' WHEN, IN TRUTH, SHE'S YOUR ENEMY."

DON.
"THE DJINN AND BAXNANS TRAFFIC IN UNTRUTHS TO KEEP YOU SOFT, WEAK.
"BUT I NEVER LIED TO YOU.

"I SHARPENED YOUR EDGE TO CUT A PATH TO TRUTH.
"WE'LL DO THE SAME FOR TARTARUS.
"TRUTH AND LIBERATION ON THE GLEAMING EDGE OF A GOLDEN RAZOR."

SIR, YOU'RE RIGHT, OTHERS MISLED ME.
BUT MY TH IN YOU REWARDED ME...
WITH HARD KNUCKLES AND A STRONG BACK.
WHEEZE BUT I CAN'T SAVE YOU FROM SELF DELUSION.

WHEN I CUT OUT GLOH'S HEART... WHEN WE BREAK THE DJINN--
WHEEZE AND BAXNA--
IT'LL BE THANKS TO YOU!

LET ME PROVE I'M NOT THAT MISGUIDED CHILD ANYMORE!
PUT YOUR FAITH IN ME.
PLEASE, SYGHUS.
POOR BOY. MY POOR, POOR BOY...

WHEEZE
YOU HAVE MY BLESSING.
BUT GO WITH TILDE AND TAKE SORM TO WATCH YOUR BACK.

YOU *WHAT?!*
THEY WERE GONNA DISMEMBER YOU!

THE DIA/VOL WAR CHEST COULD BE A LOT OF MONEY!
PRECISELY THE POINT OF A *RANSOM,* KLINZU.
WE COULD BE MAKING THEM *MORE* DANGEROUS!
IT'S THE CARD I HAD, SO I PLAYED IT.

MIGHT NOT EVEN *BE* A STASH. COULD BE JUST LORE UPPERCLASSMEN TELL EVERY INCOMING CADET.
BUT IF THERE *IS,* MAYBE THE GOLDEN RAZOR BECOMES A BIGGER HEADACHE FOR THE DJINN.
THIS COULD BE A *GOOD THING* FOR BAXNA--
TOOT TOOT!
THE *"JUSTIFICATION" BARGE* JUST PULLED IN...
AND IT *STINKS.*

WHATEVER... *INGRATE.*
WHEN DID *YOU* BECOME SO *HIGH* AND *MIGHTY?* I'M TRYING TO SAVE YOUR SKIN.
THIS IS A DANGEROUS GAME. THERE'S NO BLUFFING YOUR WAY OUT.

PROMISE ME. IF THERE'S MORE DRACHMAS THAN EXPECTED, YOU'LL TAKE THEM OUT. *MOGEN* TOO--
I KNOW HOW TO DO MY *DUTY,* KLINZU.

PLEASE, TILDE, JUST...
I *PROMISE!*

HIRSTY
NDICANT
ALE AND BRAWLHOUSE
KHARS IS DEAD. PROBABLY KLINZU AND TILDE TOO...
WE DIDN'T MEAN ANY HARM, SIR. IT'S JUST...THE FUNERAL FERRY WAS THE PLACE LEAST LIKELY TO BE CHECKED.
HIDING IN PLAIN VIEW, Y'KNOW.

BUT IT WAS WRONG. I'LL AWAIT REPRIMAND.
ASIDE FROM SCRATCHES AND BRUISES, YOU'RE HEALTHY, SOLDIER.
✓

PHLUUNCH

"REPRIMAND?"
YOU BASTARDS PUT US IN JEOPARDY. AND FOR WHAT?! FUN?! WE'RE PAST "REPRIMAND."
YOU'LL SIT BEFORE A MILITARY TRIBUNAL, SEVNO, AND STAND FOR EXECUTION.

THAT SAID.
YOU'VE GOT ONE SHOT TO MAKE THIS RIGHT, TO SAVE YOURSELF.
YOUR UNAUTHORIZED TRIPS PROVIDE VALUABLE ON-THE-GROUND INTEL. WE'RE GOING TO USE THAT TO FIND THE CLOAK.
THE CLOAK? IT'S A MYTH!
EVER WONDER WHY IT'S SO HARD TO GET HERE? WHY THE SKY ISN'T FILLED WITH JURIAN WARSHIPS?

SOME CALL IT THE CLOAK OF INVISIBILITY OR THE HELM OF DARKNESS...
I CALL IT AN ENGINEERING FEAT.

IT'S A DISTORTION FIELD, THAT SCRAMBLES THIS PLANET'S LOCATION. BUILT HERE LONG AGO.

DRAPING STYXX UNDER A UNDETECTABLE LONG-RANGE S CHARTS.

WHOEVER ATTACKED OLYMPUS MAY WANT TO DESTROY IT TOO. WE'RE HERE ALREADY, SO LET'S FIND IT AND SECURE IT.
BUT THERE'S ONLY TWO OF US! SHOULDN'T WE BLEND IN UNTIL THE RESCUE TRANSPORT COMES--

RESCUE'S NOT COMING FOR WEEKS... MAYBE LONGER. THIS CAN'T WAIT.
IT'S UP TO US. JUST US.
WHERE IS IT?

THE LEAST LIKELY PLACE, HIDDEN IN PLAIN VIEW. ALSO THE MOST HEAVILY DEFENDED PART OF TARTARUS.
YOU CAN'T MEAN...!
CHIEF, THAT'S SUICIDE!

YOU'RE ALREADY DEAD, CADET. THIS IS A CHANCE TO GET YOUR LIFE BACK.
XII

SOON.
ERVOUS, ? DON'T BE, WATCHING UR BACK.
MOGEN, YOU SHOULD KNOW THAT I REGRET...
VNNNNNN

KILLING *KATHR--*
IT'S WHAT YOU *HAD* TO DO TO SAVE YOUR CLOWNISH FRIEND, I *RESPECT* THAT.
I'VE NEVER *KILLED* ANYONE BEFORE.

YOU'LL HAVE *NIGHTMARES* AT FIRST. THE DEAD TORMENTING YOU.
YOU'LL TAKE THEM WITH YOU EVERYWHERE. LIKE OLD FRIENDS.
UNTIL THEY BEGIN TO FADE AND YOU'RE ALONE AGAIN...THAT'S THE *REAL* NIGHTMARE.
VNNNNN

FORTUNATELY, THERE'S ALWAYS SOMEONE NEW TO KILL.

HEY...NOT DOING YOUR DUTY WOULD'VE BEEN *WORSE.*
AUTO

FOR LORD-GOVERNOR OF TARTARUS
GLOH
THAT'S HIM, GLOH. HE PULLED THE TRIGGER.
BUT SURKA WAS EALLY UNDONE BY NOT VING ANYONE TO WATCH *BACK.* GOING IT *ALONE.*
VNNNNN

EVEN THE MOST DANGEROUS PERSON WALKING ONLY HAD ONE PAIR OF EYES.
BUT THERE'S *TWO* OF US, TILDE. NO MATTER WHAT THEY THROW AT US, WE'LL *SEE IT COMING* A MILE AWAY.

DIA/VOL. DERELICT WAREHOUSE.
MOGEN, YOU'RE THE *"LEFT-HANDED"* ONE, RIGHT? THE TWIN WHO WAS SUPPOSED TO DIE AT BIRTH?
YOUR POINT, SORM.
JUST 'CAUSE YOU CHEATED DEATH ONCE, DOESN'T MEAN THE UNIVERSE WON'T COLLECT WHAT'S OWED.

ESPECIALLY IF YOU'RE A DUMBASS ABOUT IT.
SORM, STAY HER
KEEP THE TRANSP
FIRED UP.
SYGHUS ORDERED ME TO--
STAY.

THIS A WILD GOOSE CHASE. BET THERE'S ***NOTHING*** HERE.
NO TRESPAS
VIOLATOR

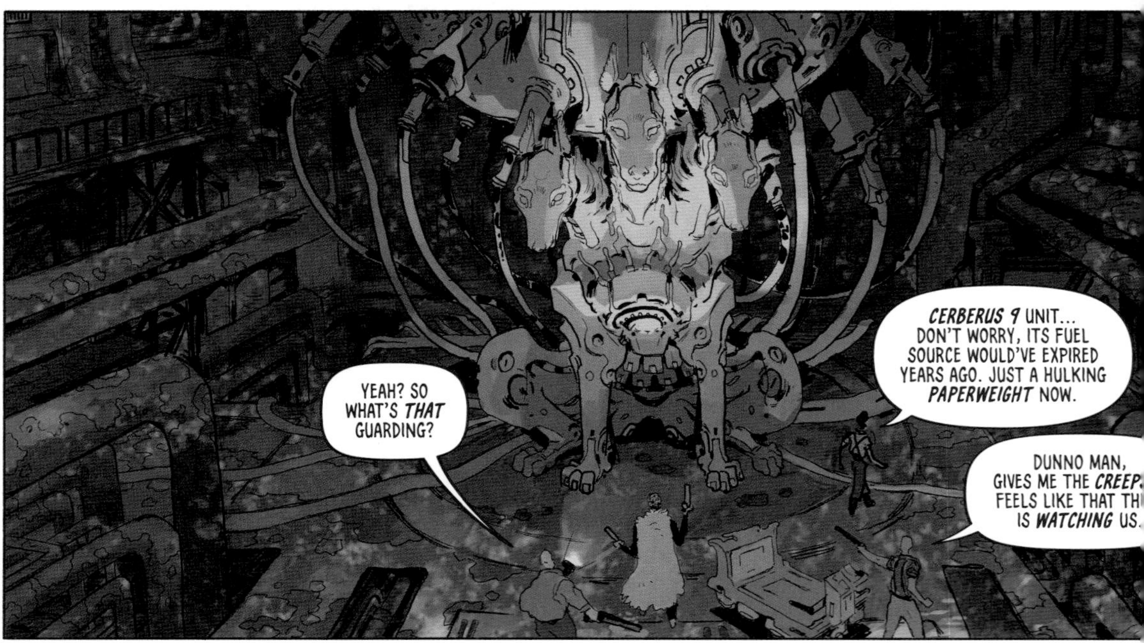
CERBERUS 9 UNIT... DON'T WORRY, ITS FUEL SOURCE WOULD'VE EXPIRED YEARS AGO. JUST A HULKING ***PAPERWEIGHT*** NOW.
YEAH? SO WHAT'S ***THAT*** GUARDING?
DUNNO MAN, GIVES ME THE *CREEP*
FEELS LIKE THAT TH
IS ***WATCHING*** US.

I THOUGHT YOU LIKED CREEPS WATCHING YOU?
ONLY WHEN I PAY THEM TO.
YOU GUYS FEEL THAT...?
HEY BOSS, TAKE A LOOK AT THIS.
HRRRMMM, MY STIMPLANT IS GOING CRAZY! I'M GETTING SERIOUS FEEDBACK...
THINK I FOUND SOMETHING.
WAIT...WAIT... GET AWAY FROM THERE...BLOOD RUSHING IN MY EARS...
I THINK IT'S COMING LOOSE!
GUYS, HE'S SERIOUS! STOP PULLING AT IT!
JUST TWO MORE SECS, IT'S ALMOST THERE...!
ARRRGHHH!
CRONK
FWWOOOSH
WE GOT IT!

ARRRGHHH!
BY THE GODDESS'S BEARD! IT'S LIQUID!

OCEANS OF IT!
WE'RE RICH! DUDE, WE'RE RICH!

THERE'S SOMETHING... DIFFERENT... ABOUT THIS LIQUID.

WE SMUGGLE EVEN HALF OF THIS STUFF AND WE CAN AFFORD AN ARMY! WE'RE GONNA LIVE LIKE PRINCES!
IT'S STILL POURING OUT, HOW MUCH LIQUID IS IN HERE?!
WE'LL BE...

UNSTOPPABLE.
NO...

MY DARKEST DREAMS OF WEALTH AND POWER...

EVERY SNUB, ANY SLIGHT AND ALL MOCKERY...

MY DISAPPOINTMENTS, NUMBERED. THOSE WHO FAILED ME, NAMED.

EVERY INSULT, ANSWERED AND EVERY HUMILIATION, REPAID.

EYE BY EYE, AND TOOTH BY TOOTH!
FWOOSH

OH SISTER. IT'S GOING TO BE A VERY BUSY YEAR!
AAAARRGH!

MOGEN! LOOK OUT!

HOOOOWWWLLLL
WHAT THE--?!
GET DOWN!

FWOOSH

HOOOWWFWINNGG
FWING
FWING

BOSS!
FWING
FWING

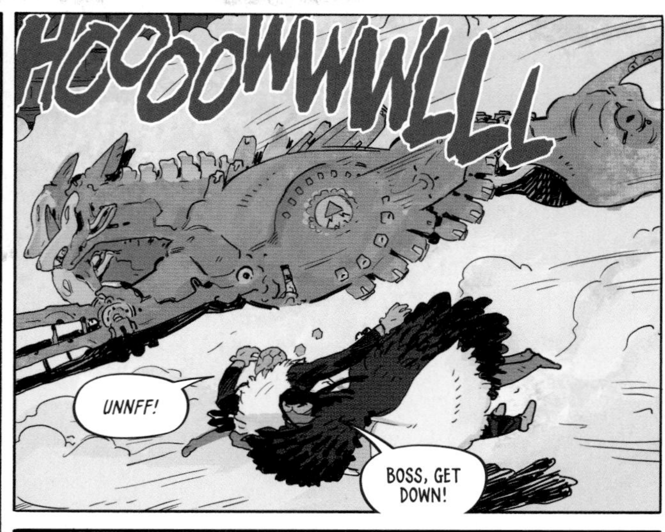
HOOOOWWWLLL
UNNFF!
BOSS, GET DOWN!

DOWN BOY!
PHWEEM

DOWN, I SAID!
KHREESH, DON'T GET BACKED AGAINST THE WALL!
PHWEEM

BAD DOG!
PHWEEM

KHREESH!
I HAVEN'T BEEN SERVICED THIS CYCLE, HOPE THIS WORKS!

REPEL.

SMASH

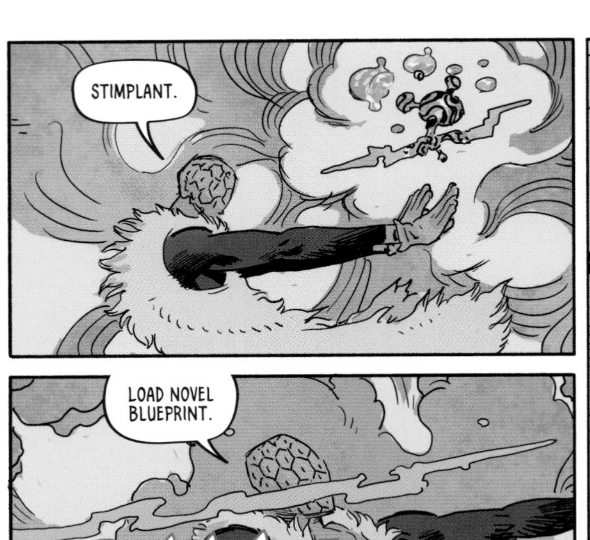
STIMPLANT.
LOAD NOVEL BLUEPRINT.
SWAAAN

CHOKE ON THIS!

SHOOOM
FWING
FWING

EMPLOY!

FWABOOM

creak
creak
WHIIINE
HWWWRRR

READY FOR ROUND TWO, PUP?!

HUP!
CRUNK

CLANG

ALRIGHT, WHERE IS IT...?

STIMPLANT. LOAD NEW BLUEPRINT. *DOUBLE TIME!*
ZZZZZRRRMM

FWING
HNF!
BOOM

HNNHH... RUSTED PIECE OF *JUNK!*

JACKPOT!
SHOOMP

ZZRRMM
STIMPLANT'S *TAXED,* NEED TIME TO *REBOOT.*
WE'RE *OUT* OF TIME...
GOODBYE, BOSS...

SHLUTCH

ZZRRMM

RRMMM

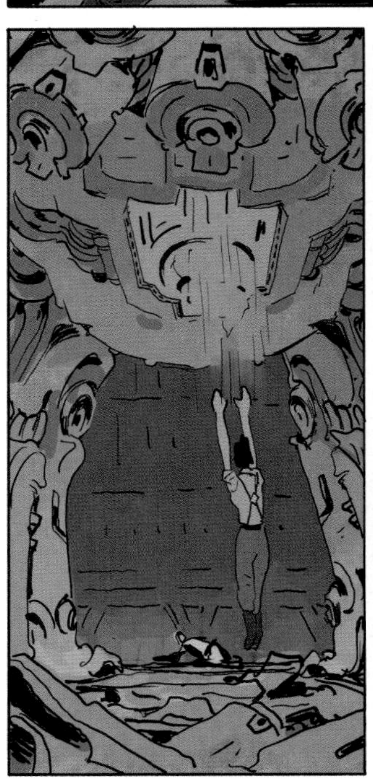

REINITIATED. WELCOME TO STIMPLANT, FULL OPERATIONAL CAPACITY IN THREE, TWO...

THANKS, SIS. I'LL TAKE IT FROM HERE.
ONE...
LOAD BLUEPRINT.

WHIIIIINE
BOOM
LIGHT IT UP!
HA!
LIKE I SAID.
UNSTOPPABLE!

SORM, BRING AS MANY OF OUR PEOPLE HERE AS YOU CAN.
OUR PRIORITY IS TO HOLD THIS LOCATION.

MOGEN, WAIT UP...

THIS IS ENOUGH LIQUID TO PAY *A THOUSAND RANSOMS.*
NOT SURE ABOUT *"A THOUSAND..."*
ENOUGH FOR ALL YOUR HOSTAGES, *PRESENT* AND *FUTURE.* NO MORE *KIDNAPPINGS,* MOGEN. NO MORE MAYHEM.

MOGEN. GIVE ME YOUR WORD THAT IT STOPS NOW.
THAT'S NOT UP TO ME, SIS.
WE DO UGLY THINGS ONLY BECAUSE WE HAVE TO--

DAMMIT, MOGEN!
MOGEN, YOU *HAVE* TO, YOU JUST... *HAVE* TO.
OK. *FINE!*

NO MORE KIDNAPPINGS.

AS FOR *MAYHEM?* THAT I CAN'T HELP.
LET'S GO HOME.

OON.
WELL YOU DID IT. ENDED THE KIDNAPPINGS--
WAS THAT A COMPLIMENT--?!
AND MADE THE GOLDEN RAZOR STRONGER.

43125
SIGH I KNEW IT...
YOU COULD'VE TAKEN OUT KEY LEADERSHIP, TILDE.
...YOU MEAN MOGEN.

HE KILLED KHARS!
HATED ARS--!
WE'RE SOLDIERS, TILDE...

WE CHOOSE OUR LOYALTIES ONCE. NOT ON A CASE-BY-CASE BASIS.
I WON'T DO IT.
I WON'T KILL MY BROTHER, KLINZU.

LIMU
I CAN'T.

BE SAFE.
YOU TOO. AND, HEY...
NOT BAD FOR A DAY'S WORK.

ELSEWHERE.
TEACH ME EVERYTHING YOU'VE LEARNED ABOUT THE DJINN.
TO FIND THE CLOAK, WE'LL BE LIKE THE CLOAK. INVISIBLE.

THE DJINN TEMPLE.
WE'RE GOING TO INFILTRATE THE DJINN.

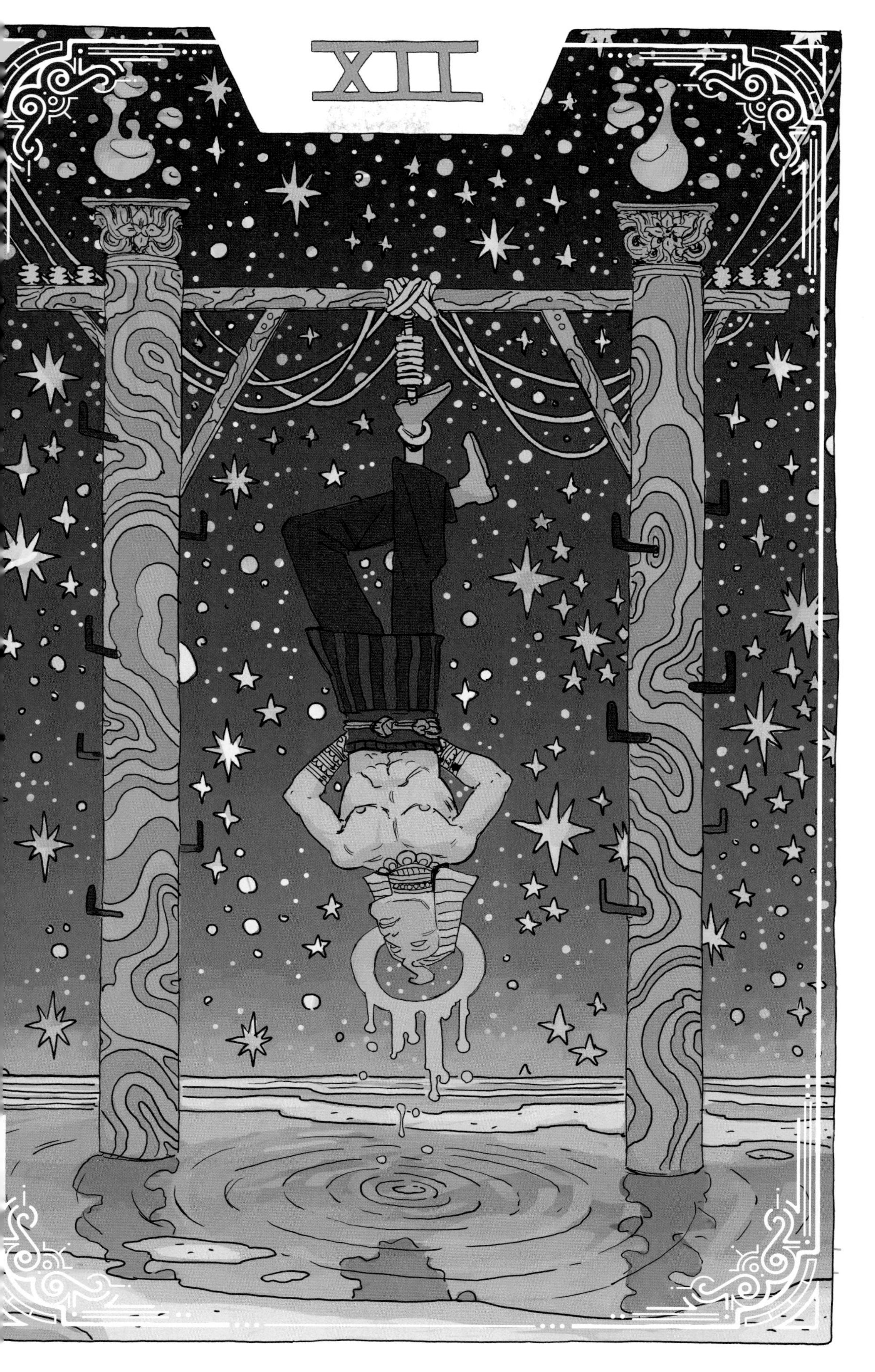
XII

CHAPTER FIVE

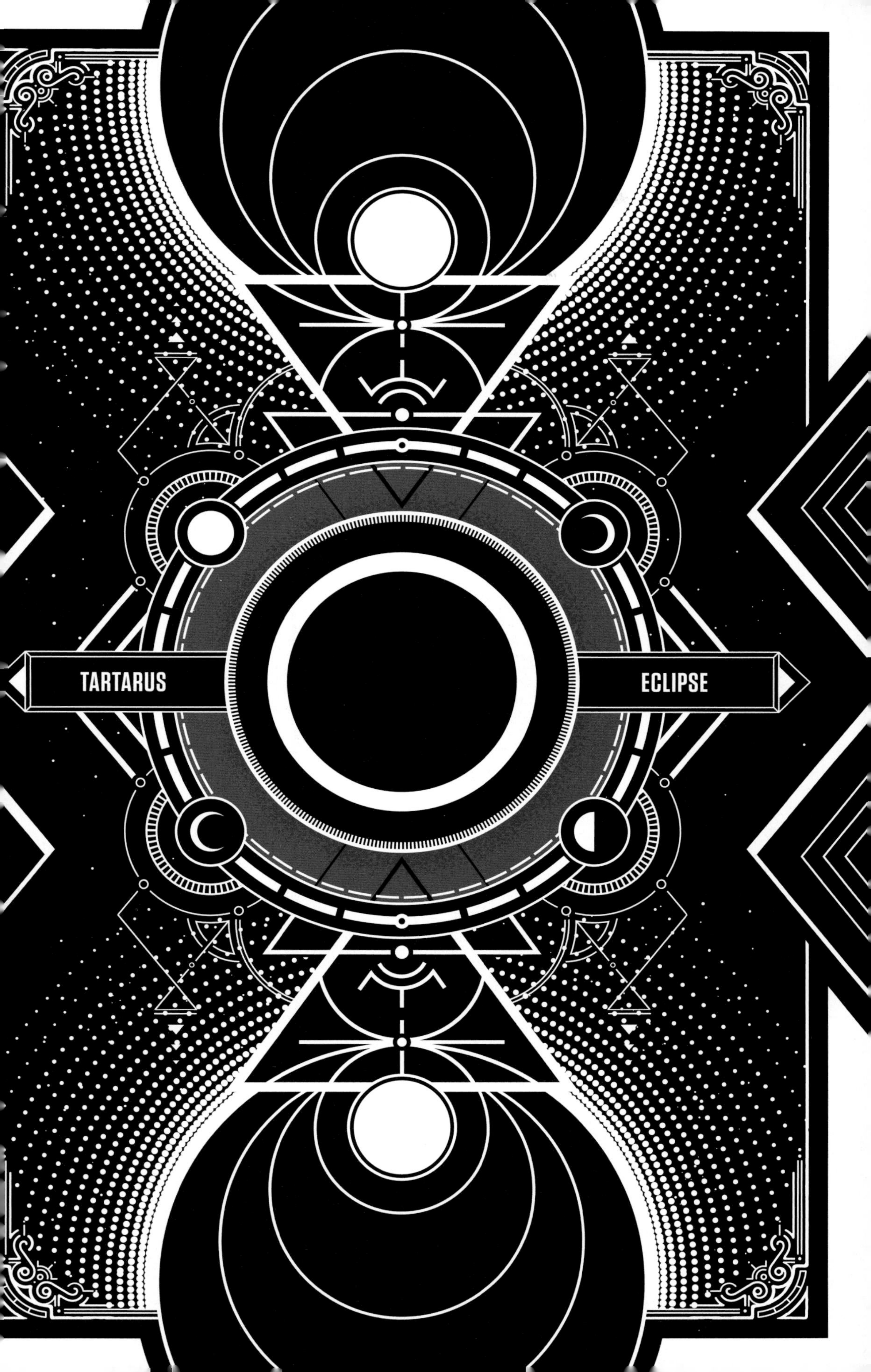
TARTARUS
ECLIPSE

EARLY WRITINGS ON THE DJINN CARTEL

from early trader/philosopher (name lost to time).

Before formal regulation in the transport and sale as sole vendors of THE LIQUID was granted (later revoked when found in duplicitous trade with our rivals in Imperium Juria).

DOSSIER ON EARLY DJINN

On Wildcat Colonia 27 are The Djinn (as they call themselves). A fascinating, highly organized, drilling and extraction institution-cum-religious order.

A strict program of religious instruction is mandatory all initiates. They then remain on the "Religious" pat may choose the Warrior's path. Thus The Djinn ar organized into these twin paths: Religious and Warr

Metallic teeth adorn high ranking religious leaders. The Most High display teeth of an unclassified Chrome-like metal. Lesser ranking members, teeth of: Gold, Silver, Mercury, Copper, Lead, Iron, Tin.

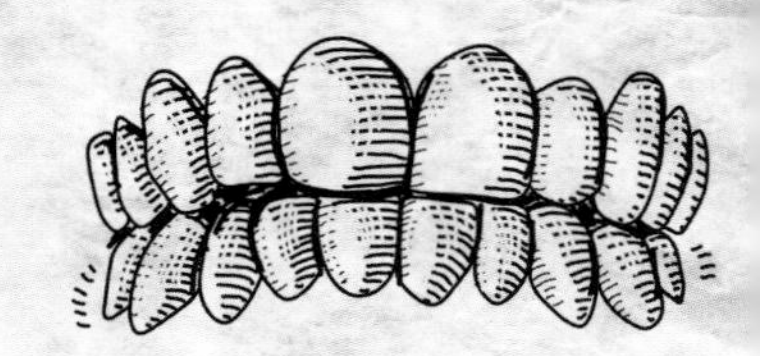

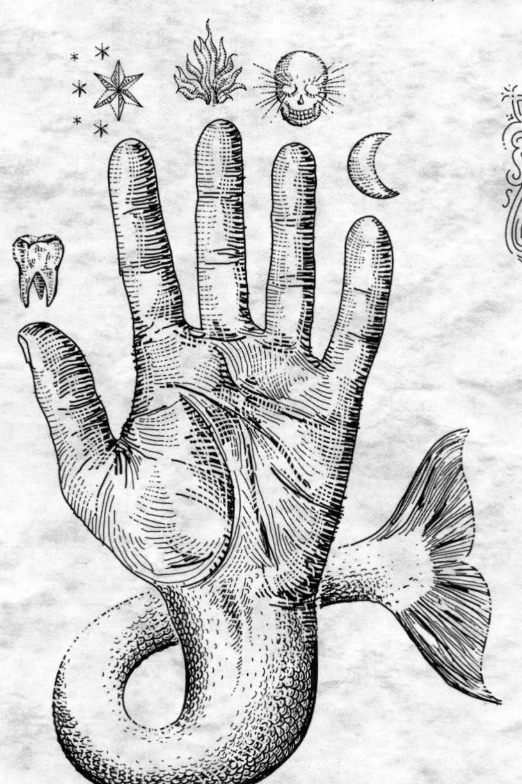

A vow of silence is taken upon initiation. Communication made only through a monastic language symbols and signs, presented in writing or by arm a hand gesture, until such time as adherents can proc their thoughts fully through The Liquid.

MOST COMMON WORDS:

- Devotion
- War
- The Sweet Water
  (Djinn name for The Liquid)
- Fecundity
- Strength of things Above
- Strength of things Below

Known to the Djinn as The Sweet Water, this infinitely malleable substance can be "blueprinted" by mental means. It is thought that advanced Djinn can communicate messages through The Sweet Water, for posterity or in real-time...

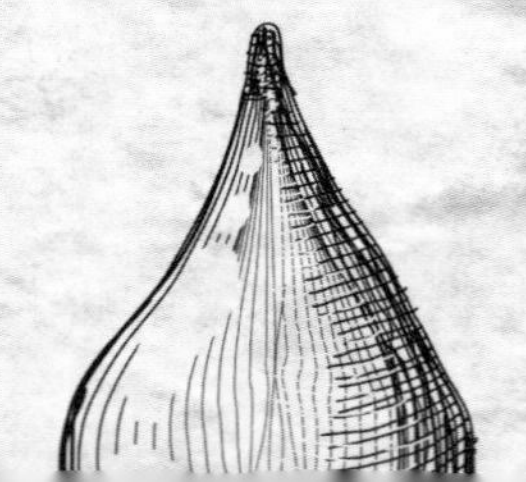

DJINN TEMPLE.
THE TRIALS OF INITIATION.
OLYMPUS STATION. DAYS AFTER THE ATTACK.
UUUUHH...
SNAP
MEDIC!

TARTARUS.
THE GOLDEN RAZOR, FLUSH WITH LIQUID WEAPONS AND SMUGGLING PROFITS, WAGE OPEN WAR AGAINST THE DJINN.

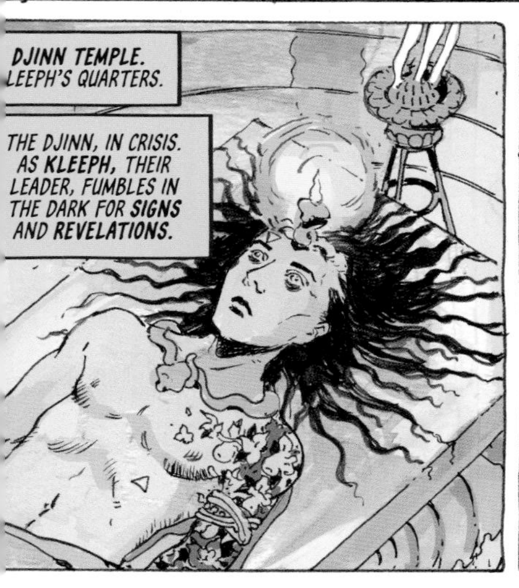
DJINN TEMPLE. LEEPH'S QUARTERS.
THE DJINN, IN CRISIS. AS KLEEPH, THEIR LEADER, FUMBLES IN THE DARK FOR SIGNS AND REVELATIONS.

BRAMBLED CITADEL. SEAT OF THE LORD-GOVERNOR.
MEANWHILE, GLOH, PUPPET RULER OF TARTARUS, HAS NEVER BEEN HAPPIER.

THE DJINN'S CALLS FOR PEACE GO UNHEARD.

AS ILZN AND SEVNO INFILTRATE THEM, IN SEARCH OF THE CLOAK.
GIVE HEED! LAY DOWN YOUR CERTAINTY AND WALK BAREFOOT INTO THE MYSTERY. WELCOME TO THE DJINN.

AND KLEEPH'S RUDDERLESS YEARS COME SUDDENLY TO AN END.
?
KNOW THYSELF
CAN IT BE?

TARTARUS.
TWO MONTHS LATER.

GASP

GOLDEN RAZOR CAMP.
DAY OF THE LONG MOON.
RABID DOG
WHEN THE COLOSSAL MOON NYX WILL ECLIPSE THE SUN, DIPPING THE PLANET IN SHADOW FOR AN ENTIRE SEASON.

A DAY OF FEASTS AND GIFT GIVING. A DAY OF TRUCE.
TILDE!

IT'S BAD LUCK TO CARRY A DEAD MAN'S WEAPON. SO I MADE YOU YOUR OWN.
A SYMBOL OF THE WAXING MOON TO LIGHT YOUR WAY AT THE START OF THIS LONG NIGHT.
BUT ARGES... I'M A TERRIBLE SHOT!

ME TOO! MY SIGHT AIN'T WORTH A DAMN.
I AIN'T MUCH OF A SIGHT FOR EYES EITHER.

BUT WITH THIS BOW, YOU AIM WITH YER HEART, NOT YOUR EYES.
THANK YOU, ARGES.

SOON.
ZYOO
HSOO
FRAK!

DIVINATION AND REVELATION

GODS DAMMIT!
"FROM THE HEART", MY EYE.

GOOD MORNING, EARLY RISER. CAN I INTEREST YOU IN A PERSONAL FORECAST? I'M QUITE GOOD.
CAN YOU TELL ME WHERE THE NEXT ARROW WILL LAND?
I'M NOT THAT GOOD...
INSIDE THE DIVINER'S TENT.
WHAT TROUBLES YOU?
NIGHTMARES.
AH. NIGHTMARES?
...OR VISIONS?

"I DON'T KNOW..."

A FORECAST IS UNWISE BEFORE A BATTLE.
SHHH!
DON'T MIND MY IDIOT DAUGHTER!
I NEED TO KNOW IF THIS ALL LEADS TO PEACE.

WAR DON'T LEAD TO PEACE.
THEN FEAR NOT. THE ETHEREAL FLAME HAS WHAT YOU SEEK.
SIGH I JUST NEED AN ANSWER.

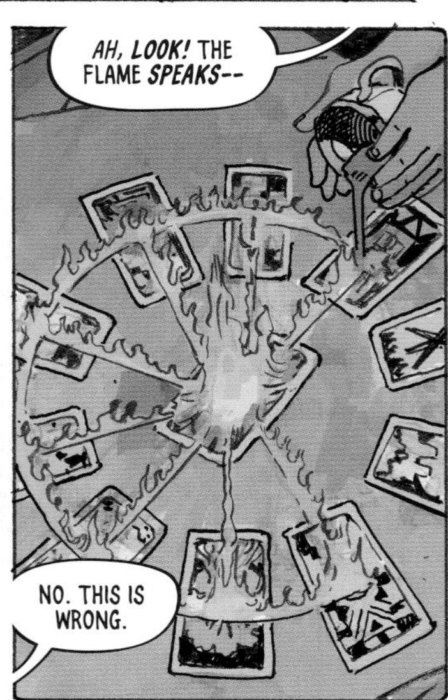
AH, LOOK! THE FLAME SPEAKS--
NO. THIS IS WRONG.

YOU CAN'T HAVE THIS FORECAST.
CLAK!

YOU'RE KIDDING... IS THIS SOME KIND OF SHAKEDOWN?
FORECASTS ARE FOR THE POWERLESS. YOU HAVE CHOICES.
DIVINATION AND REVELATION

IF YOU WANT THIS WAR TO END. STOP IT.
ME?!
THE DJINN WANT PEACE. DO YOU? OR JUST PAYBACK.

OOOM
OOOF!

THIS IS MY *BROTHER'S WAR.*
BUT YOU'RE *HELPING* HIM.
I'M JUST WATCHING HIS *BACK.* WHAT DO YOU *WANT* FROM *ME?*

TO *PROTECT* US.

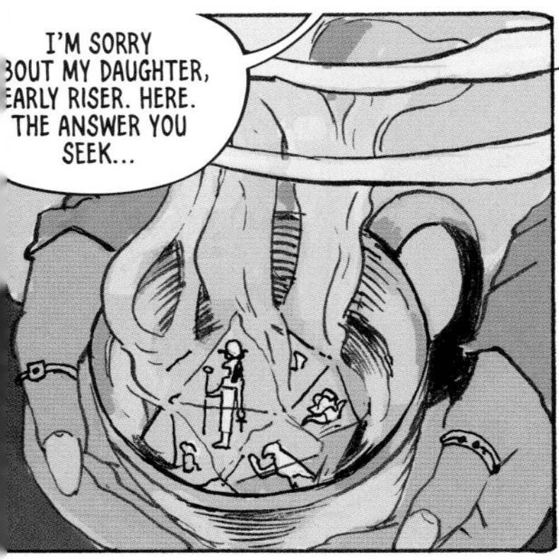
I'M SORRY BOUT MY DAUGHTER, EARLY RISER. HERE. THE ANSWER YOU SEEK...

FORGET IT.

DJINN TEMPLE.
YOU SURE IT'S THIS WAY? WE'VE BEEN HITTING DEAD-ENDS FOR WEEKS NOW.
I CAN'T HELP IT IF THE DAMNED THING CHANGES LOCATION WITHIN THE TEMPLE. PART OF ITS CONCEALMENT PROTOCOL. BUT THE CLOAK IS NEAR THIS TIME, I CAN **FEEL** IT.
WELL, MY **TRACKER** CAN.
YOU GETTING OFF ON ALL THIS?
HOW DO YOU MEAN?
YOU'VE BEEN STUDYING THE DJINN FOR A LONG TIME AND NOW YOU'RE HERE.
I'M NOT IN THE BUSINESS OF "GETTING OFF". NOT ANYMORE.
THOSE NIGHTS AS A FALLEN MAN ARE BEHIND ME.
THAT TASTE OF **SWEA** AND **AMBROSIA** DEBAUCHED OCEA BURNED AWAY B **NEW PURPOSE.**
LIQUID ENGINEERING SAVED MY LIFE.
I'VE GOT NO LOVE FOR THE **DJINN.** I STUDY THEM, ADOPT THEIR PRACTICES, TO BECOME A BETTER **ENGINEER.** THE BEST VERSION OF **MYSELF.**
TOO BAD. SOUNDS LIKE THE OLD SEVNO WAS A FUN GUY TO PAL AROUND WITH.
CHIEF, "OLD SEVNO" WOULD'VE RUN OFF WITH YOUR GIRL AFTER TAKING YOUR MONEY.
HOL' UP...
WE'RE HERE.

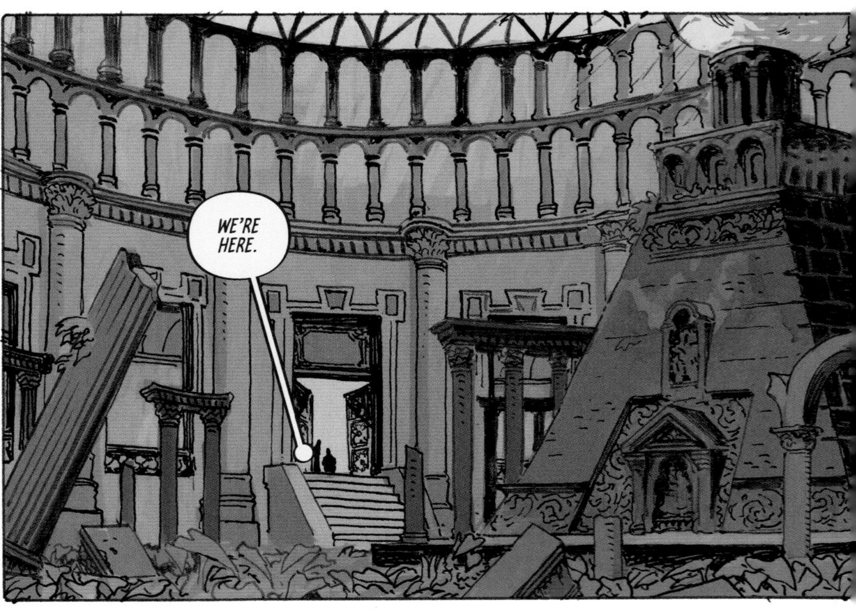

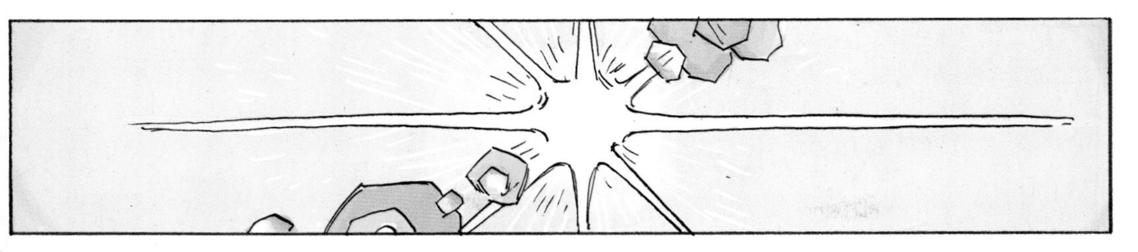

DON'T FEAR THE PRANTHA BEETLE!

ITS VAPORS WARD OFF FEAR AND BREED FRENZY!
HUFF
HUFF
HUFF

YOU'RE JOKING ME?! US, TALK TO THE DJINN? NO. WE ATTACK AFTER THE ECLIPSE AND THAT'S THAT.
SHOULDN'T WE CONSIDER THEIR OVERTURES FOR PEACE? IT BEING A DAY OF TRUCE AND ALL--

IT'S A DAY TO RAISE HELL AND PARTY HARD!
TONEE! I'M TAKING YOUR NEW CHARIOT FOR A SPIN!
UMM...HOW MUCH TUM TUM HAVE YOU HAD, BOSS?
NOT ENOUGH!

WE'D BE NEGOTIATING ROM A PLACE OF STRENGTH.
TRUST ME, CRUSHING THE DJINN HAS TO BE DONE.
I KNOW WHAT THEY'RE CAPABLE OF...YOU DON'T WANT TO GET CAUGHT IN KLEEPH'S WEB.

YEAH, MAYBE HE'LL FORCE ME TO JOIN AT GUNPOINT.
AH C'MON! YOU AIN'T STILL MAD ABOUT THAT?

BESIDES, IF THEY DIDN'T WANT WAR THEY SHOULDN'TA KILLED OUR MOM.
AND ONE DAY SOMEONE'LL WANT REVENGE FOR WHAT *WE'RE* ABOUT TO DO. WE CAN END THE CYCLE *NOW.*

ADMIT IT! YOU JUST WANNA *LEAVE*...TO GO AWAY.
YES! AS FAR AWAY FROM *HERE* AS I CAN!
I *KNEW* IT--!

KREEEUNNCHH
MOGEN!

GOTCHA!

NOT BY MYSELF, YOU JERK! ME AND YOU!
YOU... YOU WANT *ME* TO COME WITH YOU TO BAXNA?!

A FRESH START.
A QUIET LIFE ON A FARM? MAYBE THE PRIVILEGE OF SERVING ON THE GREAT OLYMPUS STATION?
YES! THAT LIFE COULD BE YOURS, MOGEN!
TILDE...

WHY WOULD I SERVE OLYMPUS, WHEN I COULD RULE TARTARUS?
WHY WOULD YOU?

SORRY, SIS. IF YOU WANNA MAKE PEACE WITH MY MOTHER'S KILLERS YOU'LL HAVE TO DO IT ALONE.
THEN I WILL.

DUDE, WHAT'D YOU DO TO MY CHARIOT?
STOP BELLY ACHING, TONEE.
TILDE, DON'T GO...YOU HEAR ME?!

DON'T TANGLE WITH KLEEPH! HE BRINGS OUT THE WORST IN PEOPLE!

HEY BOSS, I HEAR GLOH IS HOLDING COURT AT THE LONG MOON PARADE.
GLOH? THE COWARD?
GUESS HE'S FEELING BRAVE.

MORE TUM TUM!
WE'RE GOING TO THE PARADE.

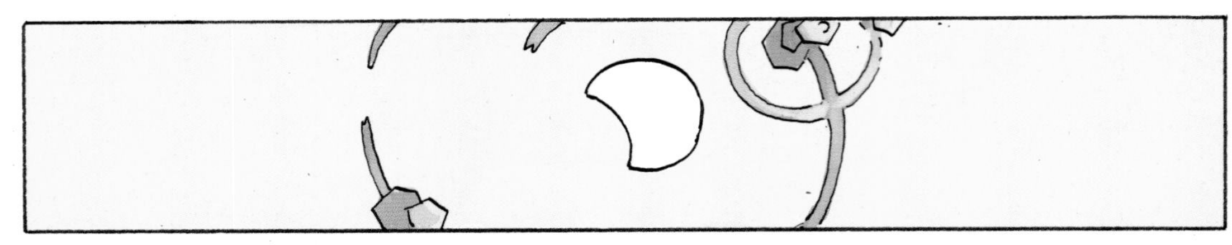

DJINN TEMPLE, MOON ROOM.
YOU SURE THIS IS THE PLACE?
ONLY WAY TO BE SURE IS TO EXPOSE THE TRACKER. I JUST NEED A MOMENT TO COLLECT MYSELF...

WHAT? WHY?
...THE SIGHT OF MY OWN BLOOD MAKES ME QUEASY.
OKAY... LET'S DO THIS.

RRRRGGHHH.

PHHFFLPAP
RRRMMMBBLLE

RRRMMMBBL

THE CLOAK OF DARKNESS.
A NAVIGATIONAL SCRAMBLER THAT MAKES TARTARUS UNDETECTABLE FROM OUTER ORBIT.
QUERY.
STATUS...

SHROUD OF NIGHT, VEIL OF STARS--
YES! YES! THE CLOAK IS STILL WORKING!

KNOW THYSELF

THROOMP

THANKS FOR FINDING MY CLOAK.
YOU HAVE NO IDEA HOW LONG I'VE SEARCHED FOR IT.
ZZHURM

ZZHURM
MY BEAUTY, YOU'VE OVERSLEPT...KEPT US IN THE DARK FOR TOO LONG.
DON'T... DON'T!
NOW SHHHHHH...

LET THE LIGHT SHINE UPON US.

DAYLIGHT.
NOOO!

OLYMPUS STATION. BRIDGE.
COMMS, WHAT THE HELL'S GOING ON DOWN THERE!
IT'S THE CLOAK, SIR. IT'S BEEN...UH... UNCLOAKED!

BULL! DOUBLE...TRIPLE CHECK THAT REPORT!

"AND GOD HELP US IF THAT'S TRUE."
SIR! YOU WON'T BELIEVE WHO'S HERE--!
I DON'T CARE...I'M LEAVING. PREPARE A SHUTTLE.

SOON.

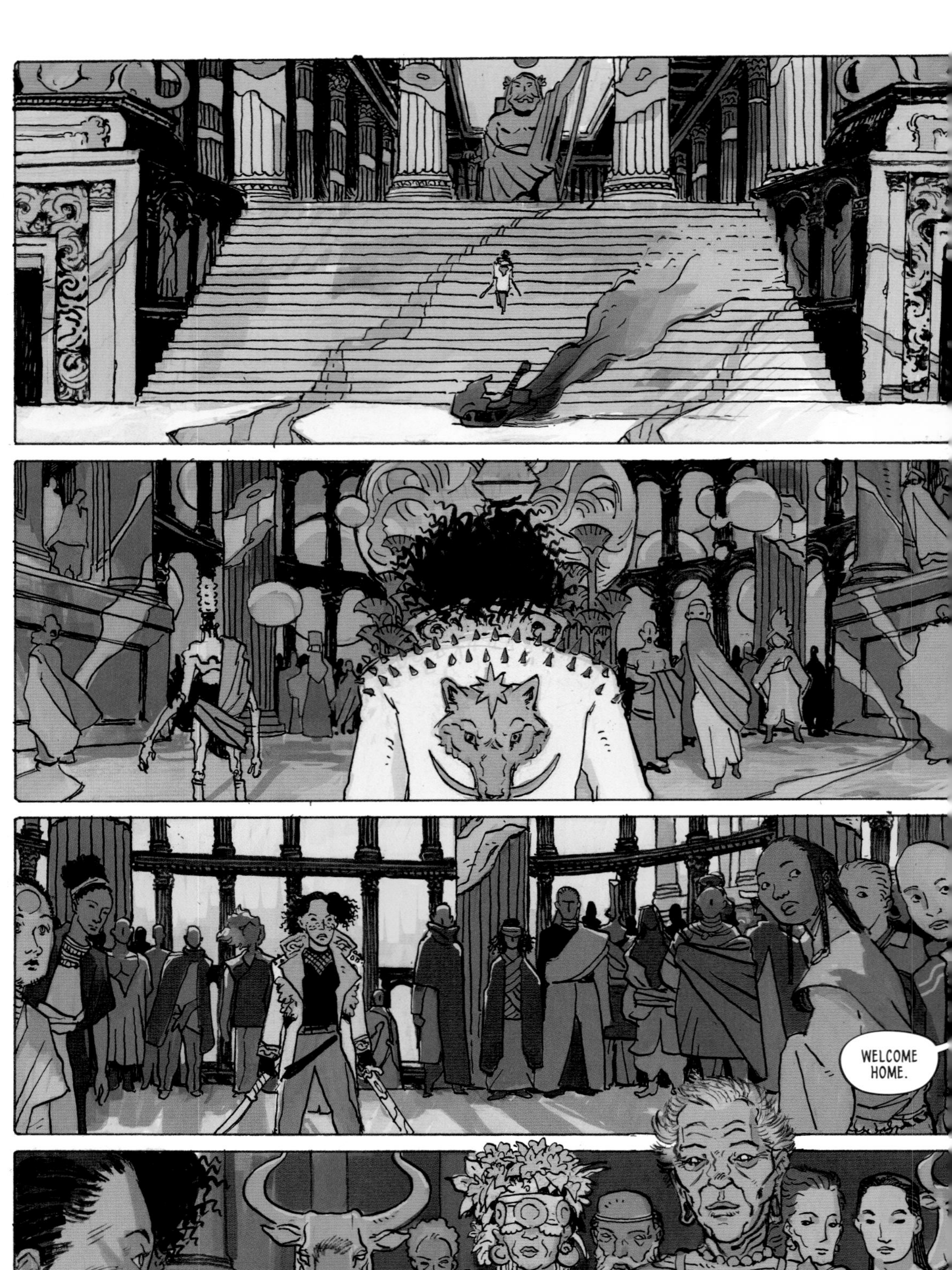
WELCOME HOME.

NOW. WE'LL TAKE THOSE WEAPONS.

THE LONG MOON PARADE.
YOU SURE THERE'RE NO SNIPERS OUT THERE?
NONE WOULD DARE, SIR. IT'S THE *LONG MOON FESTIVAL.*

LORD-GOVERNOR! TELL US HOW YOU BESTED SURKA, THE SCOURGE OF TARTARUS!
OH NOOO! THAT *OLD* TALE?!

PLEASE, LORD-GOVERNOR...FOR THE *CHILDREN!*
WELL, I SUPPOSE...

AHEM WHEN I WAS A YOUNG CADET, TWO, MAYBE THREE, CYCLES AGO.
HAHAHAHA
WELL, *PERHAPS* A BIT LONGER THAN *THAT.*
A *MONSTER* TERRORIZED TARTARUS!

I WAS JUST A COMMON SOLDIER, BUT I *KNEW* I WAS PUT THERE, ON THAT DAY, FOR A REASON.
I RAISED MY HANDS IN PRAYER AND IN THOSE HANDS, THE GODS PLACED A *THUNDERBOLT--*
SOOO FEARLESS...!
A FLASH OF *GODLY FIRE--*
SOOO BRAVE...

BUDDY, WHAT'S YOUR PROBLEM? WHO ARE YOU?
ME? I AM JUST A CHILD OF TARTARUS.

LORD MOGEN?! YOU REMEMBER THIS IS A DAY OF TRUCE AND GIFT GIVING?
I REMEMBER.

DID WE FORGET OUR GIFTS?
NO BOSS, YOU BROUGHT ONE!
OH, RIGHT, RIGHT!
THE GREATEST GIFT OF ALL!
KRASH

PEACE?!
NAAAH...

DEATH!

BIG, HARD, DEATH.

YOU'RE HERE TO KILL ME.
NO.
THEN YOU DON'T BELONG HERE.

I'M HERE FOR PEACE. TARTARUS HAS SUFFERED ENOUGH.
DOES YOUR BROTHER FEEL THAT WAY?
HE'LL COME AROUND.

JUST LIKE YOU HAVE? A LOST LITTLE MOON IN A WAYWARD ORBIT WHO'S FORTUITOUSLY FOUND HER WAY BACK?
HA! THE UNIVERSE ISN'T HAPHAZARD. IT'S A SYMPHONY OF ORDER DRIVEN BY A FORCE STRONGER THAN GRAVITY... DESIRE.
WHAT DO YOU DESIRE, LITTLE MOON?

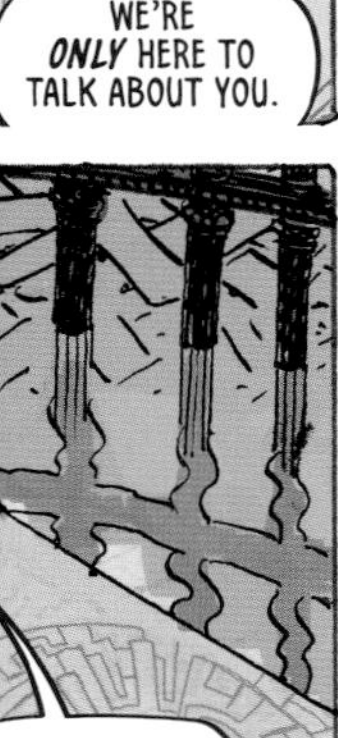

WE'RE NOT HERE TO TALK ABOUT ME.
WE'RE ONLY HERE TO TALK ABOUT YOU.

DON'T PLAY GAMES. PEACE, "YES" OR "NO", KLEEPH?
YOUR EVERY CHOICE HAS LED YOU TO ME. YOU CAME ALL THIS WAY TO FORGIVE?
I'M NARMED!

YOUR ARMS AREN'T WHAT WORRIES ME.
THERE, THAT SHOULD DO IT.
EITHER WAY, YOU'RE TOO LATE.

YOU LIKE SLAPPING KIDS, *HUH?*
MOGEN, PLEASE! THE TRUCE--
OOOF!

SHOOTING FROM THE SHADOWS? NOT SO *TOUGH* NOW?
MOGEN...ALL THOSE YEARS WITH THE DJINN...

YOU THINK I LEARNED NOTHING?
UNFF.

COCKY BOY!

GONNA WATCH YOU BURN!
ARRRGGHHH!

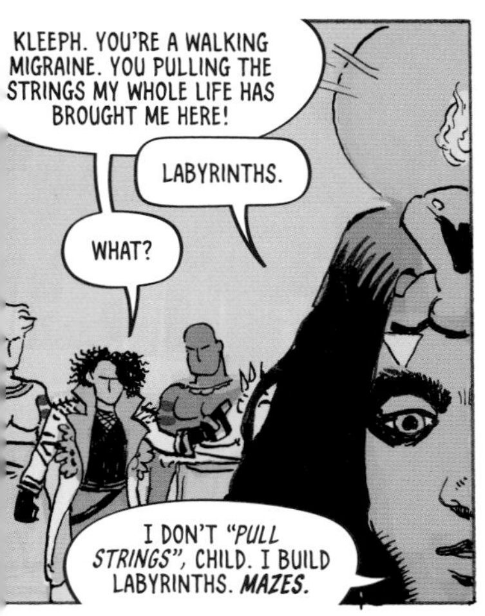

KLEEPH. YOU'RE A WALKING MIGRAINE. YOU PULLING THE STRINGS MY WHOLE LIFE HAS BROUGHT ME HERE!
LABYRINTHS.
WHAT?
I DON'T "*PULL STRINGS*", CHILD. I BUILD LABYRINTHS. ***MAZES.***

THE CLOAK WAS MY BEST MAZE. I BUILT IT TO HIDE US FROM BAXNA. BUT BAXNA GOT HOLD OF IT AND USED IT TO TRAP ***US*** INSTEAD.
BUT YOUR ILZN LED ME RIGHT TO IT. AND IT'S BEEN DESTROYED.
I CAN'T BE ALLOWED TO BUILD ANOTHER CLOAK. SO I'M DESIGNING A NEW MAZE AND TRAPPING MYSELF ***INSIDE*** IT.

ILZN?! HE'S ALIVE?!
UNIMPORTANT!

NO MORE MAZES, NO MORE RIDDLES. I NEED TO KNOW...
YOU SET UP THE OLYMPUS ATTACK DIDN'T YOU?

GETTING CLOSER.
GOT ME FRAMED FOR IT?
OOOH, ALMOST THERE.

WHY'D YOU KILL MY MOTHER?!

WRONG!
I DIDN'T KILL YOUR MOTHER.
LIAR! YOU GAVE GLOH THE BLAST CANON!

...HAHA...WELL... IT DID LOOK PAINFUL!
YOUR SWEET MOMMY, BLASTED INTO A MILLION PIECES.
BASTARD!
WE DID HER A FAVOR.

I'M DISAPPOINTED. YOU COULD HAVE ASKED WHY I OPENED THE CLOAK'S EYES. OR WHERE YOUR FATHER--
I KNOW ALL I NEED TO KNOW...

AND WHEN THAT SUN GOES DARK, I'M GONNA LIGHT YOU UP.

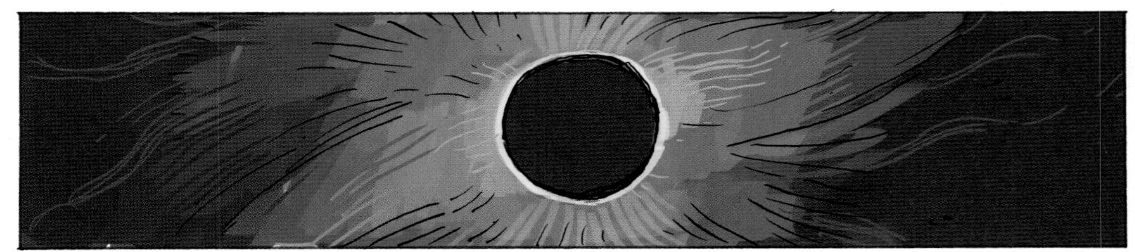

CHHHHAAAARGE!

ZYYOOOOOM

GODS DAMMIT!
ZYYOOOOOM

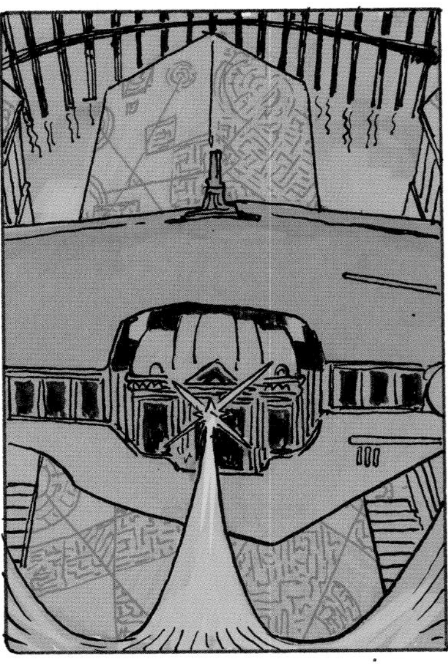

!

A CYCLOPS ARROW...? FANCY THAT...
FINALLY WE SEE... YOUR HEART'S FULL O VENGEANCE...AS DAR AS MINE.

YOU *DO* BELONG HERE AFTER ALL. BY THE WAY...

IT WASN'T A *BLAST CANON*...

IT WAS A *TELEPORTER.*

SIR. THE CLOAK IS GONE. WHAT ARE WE GONNA DO?
LEMME *THINK*, GODS DAMMIT!
"I OPENED THE CLOAK'S EYES SO *SHE* CAN FIND US."

SIR, WE'VE RUN OUT OF TIME... 'S TIME TO DROP THE HAMMER. DESTROY TARTARUS.
THOSE ARE *PEOPLE* DOWN THERE, YOU SWINE! *MY* PEOPLE.
WE KNOW, SIR, BUT...WHAT CAN WE DO?
...

...
READY THE HAMMER...
SIR, SOMETHING'S WRONG WITH THE STARCHARTS.
WHAT DO YOU MEAN?

THEY'RE GONE, SIR...
THE CHARTS? DON'T BE--
NO, SIR, THE STARS...
THE STARS ARE GONE.

OH NO NO NO! OPEN A CHANNEL TO BAXNA...!
"AND FIND US, SHE *HAS*."

THE STARS, SIR, THEY'RE BACK.
THOSE AREN'T STARS.
"REJOICE. SHE'S FOUND THE PLACE BEYOND DEATH..."

"AND HAS RETURNED..."

"YOUR MOTHER'S ALIVE, CHILD. AND ALL HELL'S ABOUT TO BREAK LOOSE!"
HISA. WE'RE HOME!
END OF VOLUME ON

II

SELECTION of JACK'S ORIGINAL CONCEPT SKETCHES

Kleeph

#1 variant cover by ***Johnnie Christmas***

#2 variant cover by **Johnnie Christmas**

#3 variant cover by ***Johnnie Christmas***

#4 variant cover by **Johnnie Christmas**

#5 variant cover by Johnnie Christmas

JOHNNIE CHRISTMAS is a #1 *New York Times* Bestselling graphic novelist based out of Vancouver, BC. Writer of **TARTARUS**, **FIREBUG** and ***Crema***. He's the co-creator and artist of ***Angel Catbird*** with celebrated writer Margaret Atwood and adapted William Gibson's lost screenplay for ***Alien 3*** into a critically acclaimed graphic novel. His credits also include co-creating **SHELTERED**.

@J_XMAS

Photo: Amanda Palmer

JACK T. COLE is an artist from Portland, Oregon who loves to write and draw scenes of the fantastic. He specializes in comics and illustration using digital means. Past projects include ***The Unsound*** and ***Epicurean's Exile***.

@NEWJACKCOLE

JIM CAMPBELL is a twice-Eisner-nominated letterer whose work can regularly be found in ***2000 AD***, and in books from Aftershock, BOOM!, Dark Horse Comics, Image Comics, Oni, Titan and Vault. He lives with his wife in a small English market town that has a pub at the end of the road. Mostly, he works from home and not in the pub. Honest.

@CAMPBELLLETTERS

STEPHANIE COOKE is a writer and editor based out of Toronto. Her debut graphic novel, ***Oh My Gods***, is out January 2021 from HMH Kids, followed by ***Paranorthern*** in July 2021. She has edited books for Image Comics, Black Mask Studios, TO Comix, Renegade Arts, and more.

@HELLOCOOKIE

Photo: Tyra Sweet

BEN DIDIER is an independent graphic designer and illustrator who had every intention of drawing his own comics before the crushing realization set in that he had no natural talent for capturing human anatomy. His graphic novel design credits include the Eisner Award-winning limited series **LITTLE BIRD** and the forthcoming **PRECIOUS METAL**, from Image Comics.

@PRETTYUGLYDSGN

Photo: David Cooper